I0602377

PAMELA FERGUSON

ii

TRUE HEARTS
A Lilac Novel
by
Pamela Ferguson

Published by Forget Me Not Romances, a division of Winged Publications

Copyright © 2018 by Pamela Ferguson

All rights reserved. No part of this publication may be resold, reproduced, stored in a retrieval system, or transmitted in any form or by any means, electronic, mechanical, recording, or otherwise, without the prior written permission of the author. Piracy is illegal. Thank you for respecting the hard work of this author.

This is a work of fiction. All characters, names, dialogue, incidents, and places either are the product of the author's imagination or are used fictitiously. Any resemblance to actual events, locales, or people, living or dead, is entirely coincidental.

ISBN: 978-1-0881-7576-7

Dedication

To my daughter, Hannah. You inspire more than you will ever know.

Chapter One

Sunny DeStefano popped open a can of Hard to Hold and doused Lavinia Burgin's bright red locks with enough hair spray to freeze a basket of slithering copperheads. She gave the styling chair a spin and smiled at Lavinia's reflection. "Sleep with a satin pillow case. Your hair will be perfect tomorrow."

Lavinia fanned the aerosol fumes with crimson-tipped fingers, diamonds flashing on her hands and wrists. "What we endure for beauty," she pronounced with a dramatic sigh, rising from the chair and glancing around the salon like a queen surveying her kingdom.

Sunny brushed off her hands and headed for the cash register before Lavinia could see her lips pull into a grin. Too bad it was only country music playing in the background and not *Pomp and Circumstance*. As the mayor's wife and owner of Lilac's only jewelry store, Lavinia had a fondness for dramatic gestures and all things sparkly.

"I see you've made some changes," Lavinia

gestured to the reception area's new curtains and brightly-colored lilac cushions. "Did your mother approve?"

Sunny bit her tongue and counted to ten. "I'm going to surprise her."

"She'll be surprised all right. These colors are definitely not Betty Sue's style." Lavinia pulled out her wallet. "You know, your parents were just a teensy bit worried about retiring and leaving you in charge. Not that you're not capable," she added hastily. "It's just that you're so young. I was thirty and married before I opened Sparkles Galore."

"Really?" Sunny's lips pulled into her polite-hair-dresser smile. Her father had been more than ready to retire to Florida after his sudden heart attack. Unfortunately, from the number of calls Sunny received from her Mom each day, it was clear somebody was having trouble adjusting to the move.

"I promised your parents I'd keep an eye on you." Lavinia wagged her finger playfully.

"I'm sure my mom and dad appreciate everything you and the mayor do for Lilac." Sunny swiped the credit card. She was getting way too much practice talking with a clenched jaw. "Are you going to Donnie and Leanne's wedding rehearsal party?"

"Of course. We try to accept every invitation. It's our duty to the residents who so kindly elected Tom into office." Lavinia lifted her chin as she surveyed her profile in the mirror. "Although, I'd be just as happy to skip this particular event."

"How come?" Sunny's brow furrowed. Donnie Greene and his bride-to-be Leanne Killian had invited the entire town to a cook-out this evening, the kick-off event for a weekend full of celebrating.

Lavinia patted her hair into place. "Don't get me wrong. I know you and Donnie's daughter Reo have been best friends since kindergarten. But just between you and me, those siblings of hers leave something to be desired."

Sunny stiffened. "What do you mean?"

"Don't pretend you don't know." Lavinia took a compact from her purse and applied some pressed powder to her shiny nose. "From what I hear, Gina's constantly moving in with different family members. Buck works in the swamps. Chris defends the worst kind of criminals. Nobody even knows where Devlin is. Carly Day's children are all as impulsive as she is."

Sunny gripped the edge of the counter, the tension from remaining silent coiling in her stomach. People were going to gossip about a woman who had five children by five different men. She knew that. But it wasn't fair that Reo and her half-siblings had to endure the consequences of their mother's choices their entire lives. How many times had Sunny been required to follow her mom's edict and stand by silently while customers traded stories about her friends?

Well, her mom wasn't running things anymore. Sunny lifted her chin. "I love Reo and her family."

"Those brothers are certainly handsome, there's no denying that. But dependable? Not in a million years." Lavinia snapped her compact shut. "Your mother used to worry you'd get involved with one of them. Don't give me that look. She almost had a cow when Buck Day invited you to prom."

"Reo's siblings are my friends," Sunny replied, her jaw tense. "As for getting involved, Reo's brothers live elsewhere. My business is here in Lilac."

"Right you are. We business owners need to stick together for the good of the town." Lavinia patted Sunny's hand. "Speaking of which, have you decided what specials the Up Do is going to offer for the two-hundred-fiftieth anniversary celebration?"

Rats! How could she have forgotten again? Her mother had called just yesterday to remind her. "I'm still finalizing my list. When do you need it?"

"By the first of July." Lavinia sighed. "You don't know how much I miss having you on the beautification committee. You were such a big help. I wish you hadn't dropped out."

Sunny missed helping the town council, too. But with Mom caring for Dad around the clock and Sunny managing the shop single-handedly, there'd been no time for volunteer work. "Maybe another time."

"I certainly hope so. We need dedicated young people like you to serve." The entrance chimes jingled as Lavinia opened the door. "Oh my, I wonder who that is." She nodded towards the shiny black sports car idling at the curb.

Sunny's jaw dropped. She'd never seen such a beautiful car. Long and low to the ground, it dominated Main Street, purring like a sleek black cat. "Wedding guest?"

Lavinia's eyes widened. "Maybe they'll be shopping for jewelry." She scurried outside.

Sunny watched as the sports car's passenger door swung open. An unexpected clash of angry shouts pierced the quiet street. Gina and Buck! She'd know those voices anywhere.

Gina, dressed in a short denim skirt and tie-dyed tank top, sprung from the car onto the sidewalk. Her brother Buck, his blue eyes blazing, leaned across the passenger seat and glared at his sister. "They're expecting us."

Gina crossed her arms. "I told you. No."

Lavinia turned around to watch the scene, eyes rounded with interest.

Uh-oh. Sunny had never seen Buck so angry. Not even the time she and Reo had filled his hiking boots with styling mousse.

Sunny ran forward and pulled Gina into her arms before either sibling could say another angry word. "Gina! How are you?"

"Sunny!" Gina sounded relieved, her slender arms squeezing Sunny tight.

Sunny motioned towards the shop. "Come on in. I'm just locking up." She waited until Gina disappeared inside the salon before leaning down to the open car door.

"What do you think you're doing?" Buck demanded.

Impatience only intensified his masculine features, making the angles of his cheekbones sharper, the set of his jaw more determined. With his long dark hair and electric blue eyes, he looked like one of those medieval warriors in the action movies her dad liked to watch.

Sunny pasted a sweet smile on her face. "You can thank me later." She waved to Lavinia.

Lavinia waved back then continued into her shop.

Buck scowled. "For what? Keeping up appearances with someone I don't give a—"

"See you at the cook out." Sunny jumped back and slammed the passenger door. The sports car revved to life and roared away from the curb. What was Buck thinking, getting into an argument with Gina right on Main Street? Didn't he know people like Lavinia craved episodes like that to gossip about?

Sunny brushed her hair out of her eyes as she entered the shop, trying to calm her pounding heart. "Hope you don't mind, but Buck just left."

Gina sat in a black leather styling chair, primping in the mirror. She waved her hand dismissively. "He does that kind of thing all the time."

Buck abandoned his sister on the sidewalk all the time? That didn't sound right. True, Buck could be ornery, and he used to disappear for days at a time when he was a teenager. When it came to his other sister, Reo, he'd always been there for her. Didn't he treat Gina the same way?

Gina spun her chair around and laughed. "I just wanted to get out of the car. We've been driving all day." With her black hair pulled back in a ponytail, Gina looked like all the other high school girls who walked past the shop window each day—bright-eyed and full of life.

"Where from?" Sunny hurried around the shop, turning off equipment.

"New Orleans. I'm living at Buck's place."

"How's that working out?" Buck had always been the silent type—except when he disagreed with someone. And he and Sunny had disagreed a lot.

Gina shrugged. "I work at the tour boat refreshment stand."

In the middle of the swamp? "You'll have to tell me about New Orleans. I've never been." Sunny threw open the door to the small rear office and scanned the desk to make sure nothing needed to be put away. She printed the register totals and counted the money while Gina took down her ponytail and combed her hair. Most of the day's customers had paid with credit cards so there was little cash to slip into the bank deposit envelope. "How about we walk to the party together? I just have to make a quick stop at the ATM."

Sunny inhaled the cool mountain air as she locked up the shop. She loved this time of the day. The sun hung low in the sky, just atop the Blue Ridge Mountains, casting Main Street in a golden glow. In a little while, when dusk fell, the Victorian-style street lamps would automatically light up, making each shopfront glisten. She scurried to the ATM next door and deposited the money.

Gina leaned against the brick wall, studying her cell phone screen while she waited.

Sunny's phone chirped. Mom's third call of the day. "Hi, Mom."

"Who's at the party?" Her mother whispered into the phone.

"Why are you whispering?" Sunny asked.

"Did Leanne's sister from Memphis show up, the one with the five-caret diamond ring?" her mother asked. "Are she and Leanne still fighting?"

Sunny blew out a breath. Mom and gossip, match made in heaven. Not. "We're just now leaving for the party."

"You and Nadine? I thought she was off today."

"Nadine was off today. I'm going with Gina." Sunny glanced at Gina and smiled.

"Gina who?" Her mother gasped. "Not Carly Day's daughter!"

"Gotta go." Sunny tapped the hang up icon. The phone slipped from her hands and clattered onto the sidewalk. She snatched up her phone, scraping her hand on the concrete. She winced.

"Is it broken?" Gina asked.

"The case is chipped." Sunny sucked on her

bleeding knuckle as she examined the damaged case. If her mother hadn't called her, this wouldn't have happened. "My mother needs to get a life!"

"What?" Gina's eyes flew wide.

Sunny blew out a breath, immediately regretting her outburst. "My parents moved to Florida three months ago. My mom still calls every day to check up on me. She keeps forgetting I'm twenty-five."

Gina stared at her open-mouthed, the click of their heels on the sidewalk filling the awkward silence.

Sunny took a deep breath as they turned the corner onto Donnie's street. Guilt coursed through her. Why was getting along with her mother still so hard? They didn't even live together anymore. "I'm sorry. I shouldn't have vented like that. My mom's okay. She just misses me, I guess." Sunny forced a smile. "Are you looking forward to the party?"

Gina wrapped her arms across her stomach. "Not really. Everyone's older than me."

"There'll be some people your age," Sunny reassured her. "I bet Donnie and Reo can't wait to see you."

Gina didn't look convinced. "Reo's married to Jack now. Donnie's getting married tomorrow."

And Gina was alone. Sunny's heart squeezed. Gina didn't have to say it. Underneath the youthful exuberance, she was like so many of the teenagers who came into the Up Do.

Uncertain about what they wanted or where they fit in. Not sure how to act. Sunny laid her hand on Gina's arm. "I'll stay with you at the party. Besides, we both have to eat."

The smell of grilling barbeque tickled Sunny's nose as they approached the neat blue and white Cape Cod. Guests of the bride and groom stood in groups on the lawn, their plates heaped with food. Her stomach rumbled as she called out to friends.

"See? You know everybody," Gina muttered, her voice sullen.

"I cut their hair," Sunny whispered as she waved. "If I'm not nice, they'll tell my mom."

Gina giggled.

"Gina!" Reo Warfield hurried across the lawn and pulled her sister into a hug.

Sunny smiled with relief as Gina relaxed into her sister's embrace. Reo was the kindest, most giving person Sunny knew. She couldn't believe almost a year had passed since Reo had gotten married. With Reo driving to Carsondale every day to teach and Sunny managing the Up Do here in Lilac, it had gotten hard to find time to spend together.

Reo extended her arms to Sunny. "Hey, Cinderella."

Sunny's lips pulled into a grin at the sound of her elementary school nickname. "Hey, Snow White," she replied automatically, as if they were both ten again.

Face lit with joy, Reo pulled her into a hug. Sunny blinked back the sudden moisture in her eyes. They lived in the same town, yet they hadn't seen each other in how many weeks?

"You two still call each other those nicknames?" Gina asked.

Reo winked at Sunny. "Once a princess, always a princess, right?"

"You said it, girlfriend." Sunny grinned as they bumped fists.

Gina screwed up her face. "That's weird."

Sunny put her hands on her hips. "Rhiannon Greene Warfield, didn't you tell your sister how we came up with those names."

Reo glanced around and lowered her voice. "I'm Snow White because I spent all my time taking care of everybody else's needs when I was a kid. Sunny is Cinderella because her parents had her working at the hair salon as soon as she could walk."

Sunny held up her hands. "Not that I minded."

"Maybe you didn't," Reo said with a huff. "You couldn't play with me because you had to sweep up hair. My stuffed animals and I were not amused."

Gina laughed. "Which princess would I be?"

Reo grasped her sister's shoulders and eyed her up and down. "Sleeping Beauty, because you don't see how beautiful you are inside and out."

"I'm not beautiful," Gina protested, dipping her chin.

Reo spread her hands. "See what I mean? What do you think, Cin?"

"Definitely. Sleeping Beauty." Sunny pulled out her phone and aimed it at the three of them, amazed by Reo's knack for always knowing the right thing to say to cheer someone up. "To commemorate our royal reunion." She snapped a selfie of their three smiling faces.

Reo's husband, Jack, suddenly appeared behind his wife on the tiny screen. "Me, too." He planted a kiss on the top of Reo's head as he slipped an arm around her waist. Sunny felt that sudden tug of yearning that hit whenever she was around couples who were so obviously in love. Reo and Jack were head-over-heels crazy about each other.

Sunny tried to focus on taking the picture. In the background of the selfie, she watched Reo's oldest brother, Chris, sprint across the lawn towards them.

"Don't forget me." Chris slid his lanky frame in between his sisters, bumping them each playfully on the hip. "How's it going, Sunny? Last time I saw you, you had purple hair."

Sunny laughed, relaxing into the warm feelings that Reo's family always stirred in her. "Thought I'd better tone it down for the wedding."

"That's code for better not tick off the bride, right?" Chris stretched his neck and turned his head as if he were looking to see if Leanne was in earshot.

Reo poked Chris in the side. "Sh."

"I'm the oldest. I can get away with it." Chris turned around. "Hey, Buck, get over here."

Sunny glanced over her shoulder. Buck stood talking with Donnie, his expression serious. He made a final comment to his stepfather and sauntered across the lawn.

Gina's smile faded as Buck approached. Sunny tightened her arm around Gina's shoulders, protectiveness surging through her. What was going on between Gina and Buck?

"Where do you want me?" Buck drawled.

"Stand next to Sunny," Chris commanded.

"Do I have to?" Buck asked.

Sunny pressed her lips together. She could take a hint. "I'll step out and take the picture. You guys are all family."

Buck's hand on her arm stilled her. "I was teasing." His lips eased into a smile. "Go ahead and take the picture."

A tingle shot across her skin where he touched her. Sunny glanced to her left. If she stepped away, Gina would be standing next to Buck, something Gina obviously didn't want to do. Sunny pasted a smile on her face. "Okay, on three." As everyone huddled closer, Sunny suddenly felt Buck's muscled arm around her shoulders. Her heartbeat skipped as she leaned against him, her cheek bumping his chest as his spicy scent washed over her.

"One, two, three," Sunny said, steadying her shaking hand. She snapped the picture.

Everyone gathered around to see the photo. Everyone except Buck. Without a word, he released Sunny and disappeared into the crowd.

So, he was still mad at her for interfering earlier.

"Hey, Gina, stop talking so much." Chris laughed as he lifted Gina into his arms and spun her around, making her squeal in surprise. "Race you to the food."

Sunny laughed as the two took off across the lawn. Thank goodness, Gina got along with her other brother Chris.

Reo gave Sunny's arm a playful poke. "Did you see my text? I don't have shoes to match the bridesmaid dress."

Jack slipped his arm around Reo and grinned. "You mean the pink cloud?"

"That's the polite name for it." Reo scrunched up her face, and Jack pulled her close, laughing. "Layers and layers of pink all puffed out to here." Reo spread her arms wide. "Anyway, can I borrow a pair of black patent sandals?"

Sunny crossed her arms and tapped her foot. "Sure, if you explain why you didn't tell me you're pregnant."

Reo pressed her hand to Sunny's mouth. She shot a worried glance at Jack. "I *told* you she'd know." She lowered her hand. "Promise you won't tell anyone. I don't want to upstage Dad's wedding."

"Congratulations!" Sunny whisper-squealed, pulling them both into a hug. "You mean upstage your future stepmother. Good choice. Here she comes."

"We're hungry." Reo tugged Jack's hand,

pulling him away.

"Cowards," Sunny mouthed as they disappeared into the crowd.

The hem of Leanne's long floral skirt brushed the grass as she glided among the guests, making it look like she was floating across the lawn. Sunny held her breath as she studied the elaborate honey-gold up do she'd created for Leanne that morning. Still intact. Thank goodness she'd used both gel and hair spray to keep Leanne's hair under control.

Leanne squeezed Sunny's hands, her green eyes bright with purpose. "Thank you so much for agreeing to style my attendants' hair tomorrow. I don't know what I'd do without friends like you."

"I'm looking forward to it." Flowers. Dresses. Food. Photos. For almost a year, Leanne had agonized over every detail, determined her wedding would be stunning. It may have been Donnie's second wedding, but it was Leanne's first, and she wanted everything to be perfect. She'd wanted to hire wedding service providers from Charlottesville, but Donnie had put his foot down. Lilac businesses only. Sunny would never hear the end of it if she spoiled even one tiny aspect of the celebration. Not to mention what her own mother would say.

Leanne's pink lips stretched into a smile, her expression sugar-sweet. "Would you be able to do me one more favor?"

Why was Leanne holding her hands so

tight? Sunny resisted the urge to step backwards. "Sure. What?"

"Give Donnie and Buck haircuts tomorrow morning."

Sunny's jaw dropped. "I thought Donnie was going to the barber shop."

"That was the original plan. Now that Buck is staying with Donnie, I thought you could drop by the house and kill two birds with one stone."

Sunny shot a glance across the lawn to where Buck stood talking with Tom and Lavinia Burgin. Her gaze narrowed. She couldn't believe Lavinia, smiling pleasantly at Buck as if she'd never said those mean things about him at the salon. Buck's full lips curved ever so slightly. Was he amused at something the mayor said, or laughing at the mayor himself? She could never be sure with Buck. Her gaze lingered on his proud stance, the long dark hair curling over his collar, the shadow of a beard on his chin.

As if sensing her scrutiny, he glanced at her. One eyebrow lifted in silent acknowledgment.

Sunny looked away, her palms suddenly sweaty. "Buck doesn't want a haircut, does he?"

"No, he doesn't." The sweetness had drained out of Leanne's voice, replaced by an I-can't-believe-this-is-happening-the-night-before-my-wedding tone. "There are photographs to consider." Leanne released Sunny's hands and walked away.

Sunny turned on her phone and texted herself a reminder: duct tape. It wouldn't be the first time she'd used it on Buck.

~

Bright and early Saturday morning, Buck stood barefoot in his stepfather's kitchen, wishing for the thousandth time in his life that Sunny DeStefano would go away. How could anybody be so cheerful, so optimistic? She reminded him way too much of things he'd never have.

She stood waiting for him just beyond the screen door, hair clippers pointed straight at his heart. "You. Sit."

The morning sun streamed onto the back porch where Sunny had set up a chair for barbering. The scent of lilac rode the breeze, dousing the Virginia mountain town in its annual explosion of sweetness. He closed his eyes and inhaled. He hadn't realized how much he'd missed it. Not much lilac in the swamp.

"I'm waiting." Sunny's sandal-clad foot tapped the floor boards, her silver anklet twinkling in the sunlight. Her short, black skirt revealed a pair of long, tanned legs, muscles taut with impatience.

"Ought to be a crime to ambush a man this early in the morning." Buck pushed his tangled hair out of his eyes and cast a lazy look at his stepfather. "Let me guess. The bride wants me to get a haircut."

Donnie sat reading the newspaper at the other end of the porch, his salt-and-pepper hair trimmed up neat. He nodded without looking over. "Yep."

Silver bangle bracelets clinked together as Sunny crossed her arms over her frilly white top, her glossy dark hair spilling over her shoulders. "Leanne does not want you photobombing the pictures with your swamp dog look. Be a good usher and do what she wants."

Buck ran a calloused hand down his bristled jaw. "Folks expect a Louisiana swamp boat owner to look the part, *chere*."

Donnie chuckled. "Tourists buy that fake Cajun accent?"

Buck grinned. "Yes, if the tips are any indication."

Sunny blew out a breath. "I have a long list of clients today. Are you going to let me cut your hair, or do I have to call the bride?"

A look of panic flashed on Donnie's face. "Better do what she says."

Buck had been back in Lilac less than twenty-four hours, and the tension around Donnie's house was thicker than bayou fog. Of course, Donnie and Leanne had brought it on themselves by inviting the entire town to the celebration.

Buck sighed, shoved his hands into the pockets of his jeans, and sauntered onto the back porch. If he ever got married—*not* that he had any plans of ever getting married—he'd do it up simple like Reo and Jack. Immediate family and a couple friends. Quiet ceremony. Lunch afterwards. Thinking about the three-ring circus he was about to be a part of made him want to hop in his car and disappear. Thank God, tomorrow this time he'd be on the road, heading back to New Orleans. All of this would be a memory.

The old wooden chair creaked as he sat down.

Sunny snapped open a large towel and draped it across his chest. "Hard to believe you let me pretend-shave you with a butter knife when we were kids."

"For a price." He stretched out his legs and slanted a pointed look up at her.

Sunny rolled her eyes. "Are you referring to that sorry kiss you planted on me when I was all of twelve? Please." She motioned Donnie over and handed him her phone. "Okay, Mister Groom, make yourself useful. Take a picture of Buck and me doing the deed. We'll send it to Leanne and make her laugh."

Sunny turned on the clippers and aimed them at Buck's head.

Buck's hand shot out and circled her wrist, the electric clippers buzzing between them. Vibration rattled up his arm as her wide-eyed gaze locked with his. He shook his head. "No clippers."

Flash! "Got it!" Donnie said.

Sunny snatched the clippers from his grasp with a huff.

Donnie showed them the image and laughed. "Looks like you two want to kill each other."

The corner of Buck's mouth curved.

"Sounds about right."

Sunny had been a fixture around the Greene home for as long as Buck could remember, his half-sister Reo's best friend since kindergarten. The girls' endless giggling used to drive him outside faster than any recess bell. Seeing Sunny last night in the moonlight, he couldn't deny she'd grown into a beautiful woman. There'd been a time when he'd thought there might be something between them, but that had been a foolish teenager's dream.

"I'm leaving you two alone against my better judgment." Donnie pointed at the back yard. "Promise I won't find one of you tied to that tree when I get back."

Buck snorted. "That was fifteen years ago. Today I'd just lock her in a closet."

Sunny batted her lashes at him. "Not before I cut off your ear."

"Surrender, Buck. She's armed." Donnie chuckled. "Thanks for the haircut."

"My pleasure." Sunny gave Donnie a hug.

Donnie paused as he pulled open the screen door. "Sorry your parents couldn't make it up for the wedding. Give them my best."

"I'll do that."

Buck tilted his head. Sunny's parents had been fixtures around town forever. The perfect Lilac family. "Where'd your parents go?"

Sunny lifted sections of his hair and examined them. "Florida."

"Leaving you in charge of the salon?"

"You got it." She tugged a lock. "When's

the last time you cut your hair?"

Buck shrugged. "Who knows? Wouldn't be cutting it now if I'd stayed home."

Sunny dropped the hair she'd been holding. "Don't you want to be in Donnie's wedding?"

"Sure, for Donnie. Just not a big fan of marriage." His own mother had five children by five different men and had married all of them except Buck's father Spike.

He scowled at the sudden flash of sympathy on Sunny's face. As a kid he'd gotten good at dodging Lilac residents who offered pity to his face when they weren't gossiping behind his back. Poor Buck Day. Abandoned by his father and his mother. What a shame.

"This dress looks like a bag of cotton candy." The screen door banged open and Gina stomped out of the kitchen onto the back porch, her puffy pink dress bouncing around her knees like a balloon. "I told you I didn't want to do this. Oh. Hi, Sunny."

Great. Pity and complaining. This day was going to be even more stressful than he'd predicted if things didn't lighten up. Buck took a deep breath. "You look nice."

Sunny stepped forward to give Gina a quick hug. "Aren't you excited about being in the wedding, S.B?"

Buck's brow furrowed. "Who's S.B.?"

"Sleeping Beauty," Sunny replied, her pert little nose in the air. "He wouldn't understand, would he, S.B.?"

"No, he wouldn't." Gina shot Buck an

irritated look. "I would be excited if I could've invited Remy."

"Who's Remy?" Sunny asked, her questioning gaze shooting between Gina and Buck.

"We've been over that." Buck regretted his curt reply as soon as the words were out of his mouth. Why was he finding it so hard to be patient? He had to keep reminding himself Gina was only a kid. "Did you talk to your father yet?"

Gina scowled. "No." She turned to Sunny, her expression dreamy. "Remy is one of the tour boat captains. He's really cute. I wanted to invite him to the wedding, but Buck said no."

Buck fought to keep his voice calm. "He's way too old for you."

Gina lifted her chin in the air. "When I'm eighteen there'll be nothing you can do about it." She ran into the house, the screen door banging shut behind her.

Sunny set down her comb. "What's so bad about Remy?"

Buck crossed his arms. "Did Leanne hire you to cut hair or gossip?"

"Hello? Have you forgotten who discovered you even had a second sister?" Sunny planted her hands on her hips.

"That gives you the right to gossip about her?" Buck clamped his jaw tight before he said something he'd regret. He'd never forget how embarrassed he'd felt the day his sister Reo dragged eight-year-old Sunny upstairs to his bedroom and made her repeat the whispered gossip she'd overheard at the Up Do. His mother Carly Day was living twenty miles away in Carsondale. She was married again with a daughter—her fifth child—and hadn't even thought to pick up the phone and tell her other four children.

"So, I care about Gina. Sue me." Sunny went back to combing his hair.

Buck shifted his shoulders, trying to settle into the hard-backed chair. "You don't hear me asking why your parents moved to Florida. Ouch!"

Sunny's comb pulled at a knot. "They retired."

"Always pegged them as Lilac lifers." The comb scraped his scalp and stuck in a tangle. "Hey!" He angled his shoulders sideways, sliding his hair from her grasp. "How about a shampoo?"

"How long will it take you to shower?" Sunny glanced at her cell phone.

Buck rubbed the back of his neck. "Can't you wash it?"

The corner of her mouth curved. "And give you a nice scalp massage, I suppose?"

He arched an eyebrow at her. "Give you a big tip."

Sunny snatched a bottle of shampoo from her supply bag and marched into the kitchen, letting the screen door slam behind her. "Come here."

He followed her into the kitchen. "You're

kidding."

She leaned her hip against the sink. "Well, I'm not climbing in the shower with you."

"Why not? We went to the swimming hole together," he said.

"Don't act like it was anything special. Half the kids in town were skinny-dipping that night." Sunny got up on tip-toe and draped the towel across his back, her fingers cool on his neck. "Bend over."

He glanced over his shoulder. "In another context, that comment could be construed as sexual harassment."

Sunny narrowed her gaze. "Do I have to get the duct tape?"

"You're even bossier than you used to be." He lowered his head into the sink, his back muscles cracking with relief as he stretched forward. Closing his eyes as warm water coursed through his hair, he relaxed into the heat, feeling the tension drain out of his neck muscles. He couldn't remember the last time he'd had a scalp massage.

A sudden blast of hot water singed his head. He jerked to the side. "Hey, watch it!"

Sunny stared at him, brown eyes wide with innocence. "Too warm?"

"What are you, ten? Fix the temperature." He blew out a breath as the water cooled down.

Her phone buzzed. Out of the corner of his eye Buck watched Sunny reading a text message. "Mrs. Merriweather wants me to style her sister, too." She poured on the shampoo and lathered it up. "Do you remember her? She used to live in the big blue house on Madison Street. Her husband just retired from some big airline. He was a pilot."

Buck closed his eyes, lost in the tingly feeling of her fingers kneading his scalp. "Could you please stop talking?"

"Most clients like me to talk. You don't have to talk back, Mr. Big Tipper." She squirted his face with the sprayer.

Water dripped down his nose as she rambled on. Donnie should've warned him the price of a haircut was listening to gossip. He wished he could close his ears as easily as he could close his eyes.

"Mrs. Merriweather says she wouldn't know what was going on in town if I didn't come to the Mountain Mist senior community to cut hair. Mr. Deutsch calls me his little ray of sunshine. Remember Dewey's dad? He's in the early stages of Alzheimer's." Her fingertips scrubbed hard as she rinsed out the lather. "Mr. Quisenbury's the only one who doesn't like to talk much."

Buck's body tensed. "Mr. who?"

"Mr. Quisenbury."

Buck jerked upright, whipping his head out of the sink. Water streamed down his face.

Sunny shrieked and jumped back. "You got me all wet!"

He grabbed a dishtowel and dried his face. Water ran in rivulets beneath his tee shirt, all the way to his bare feet. A shiver ran down his back. "Mr. Quisenbury. What's his first name?"

Sunny looked at him like he was crazy. "Norton. No, wait. Norbert."

"How old is he?"

"Eighty-something. Why?"

Figure the odds. The senior community. Donnie had said something about the new facility, but Buck had never thought of looking there. He rubbed the towel through his wet hair, his heart pounding. Eighty was way too old. A distant relative of his father's?

Buck strode outside onto the back porch and dropped into the chair. Most folks had only known his father as Spike, a wandering biker who'd swept Carly Day onto the back of his Harley and sped into the sunset. Very few people in this town knew his father's real name.

Norel Quisenbury.

Buck had accepted long ago there'd be no joyous reunion with the man who'd only stayed around long enough to give Buck his DNA and a nickname. Their last short encounter a decade before had been painfully awkward. Yet, the need to know more about the man who'd fathered him ran deep in his bones, leaving a gaping hole in a place that might have held family pride.

"I'll see you at the reception." Sunny's voice drifted through the screen door.

"Wait!" He yanked open the door and hurried into the kitchen.

Sunny sat with her back to him, dark hair draped over one shoulder, her phone pressed to her ear.

Buck cleared his throat. "Um, my hair."

"Just a minute." She angled her head over her shoulder, hand covering her phone. "You need to clean up your mess." Her pointed gaze dropped to the wet floor, her tone all business. "What were you saying, Phil?"

Buck ripped paper towels from the roll and threw them onto the puddles around the sink as Sunny continued her conversation. Sometime during the past few years that irritating schoolgirl giggle had changed into a woman's laugh, warm and inviting. The kind of laugh a man wanted to hear on a cold winter night.

"You're kidding!" she exclaimed. "I can't wait to see it."

Buck wiped up the linoleum and tossed the wet paper towels into the trash, searching his memory for Lilac residents named Phil. He drummed his fingers on the counter, waiting for her to hang up. "Who's Phil? And what's he got that you can't wait to see?"

"Ha-ha." Sunny stood, smoothing her hands over her skirt. "You'll meet him tonight. He's an engineer at the solar energy plant."

"What does he want to show you? His big house or his new car?" Seemed like all the women he met these days had dollar signs in their eyes. Could women in Lilac be any different?

Sunny's gaze narrowed. "As a matter of fact, neither. He's restoring a vintage Mustang and wants me to see the new paint job."

"Right." Buck snorted. "Are you going to cut my hair or not?"

"Not." She glanced at the clock. "Your time's up."

"What about the wedding pictures?" he sputtered.

"Should've thought about that before you started insulting me. I told you I had clients waiting. It's not my problem you refused to listen." She strode out of the kitchen onto the back porch.

Buck gripped the counter. Uh-oh. For all his griping, he really didn't want to ruin the photos. Donnie didn't deserve that. He jogged onto the porch where Sunny was packing up her supplies. "Don't leave."

She threw her bag over her shoulder and walked past him, eyes straight forward. "Shave. Pull your hair into a ponytail. You own a swamp boat. Folks'll understand."

~

Sunny jammed the key into the ignition of her lime green VW Bug, her gaze fixed on the small silver cross clipped to her visor. *Please, God, give me patience.*

Why did Buck bring out the worst in her? They went at each other like cats in a bag. He accused her of gossiping about Gina, implied she liked Phil for his money. What had she done to deserve that? With everyone else, she could keep her thoughts to herself, say the right things, like the Little-Miss-Customer-Service her mother had raised her to be. Being around Buck removed all her filters. Words spilled out of her mouth before she could control them.

Thank goodness, he never came into the salon. There, she had to watch every word she said for fear of offending a client. Her dad had said more than once that being in business meant being a diplomat.

She glanced in the mirror, blinking away the moisture that threatened her mascara. What in the world had made Buck jump and splash water all over her? It was like he'd been struck by lightning. She'd had clients tell her they sometimes got their best ideas when Sunny was massaging their scalps, but Buck's reaction was ridiculous. She pressed a tissue to the damp spots on her blouse. Her clients expected her to be fashionably dressed, with perfectly styled hair and flawless makeup. If she walked into her next appointment at Mountain Mist with wet clothes and raccoon eyes, she'd never hear the end of it. *You are a walking advertisement for the Up Do salon,* her mom always said.

Her mother. She would have a fit about Sunny wasting her time arguing with Buck on the morning of a wedding. There was still the bridal party to style, not to mention attaching Leanne's veil. Sunny's phone rang.

"Where are you?" Jill Vogel, the event coordinator from the Mountain Mist retirement community, asked. "Every five minutes somebody wheels over to the counter and demands to know when you're coming."

Sunny cringed. "Please tell me you're

joking."

"Of course, I'm joking." Jill chuckled. "Some of your clients are getting antsy, though. They insisted I call and make sure you're not broken down on the side of the road. You brought this on yourself by always being early."

She glanced over her shoulder at Donnie's front door and nibbled her bottom lip. Leanne would never forgive her if Buck showed up with a sloppy ponytail. "Give me twenty minutes."

"Okay, but hurry. The residents want to get to the church early and catch up on all the gossip."

Sunny climbed out of the car, supply bag gripped tightly in her hand, and marched up Donnie's front walk. She was the manager of the Up Do. She needed to keep her word to Leanne, even if it meant putting up with Buck's obnoxious behavior. Just because he was disagreeable didn't mean she had to be.

She glanced up at the bright blue sky. "You can help me do this," she whispered. Ever since her parents had moved away, Sunny had found herself asking God for help a lot more frequently. *Trust in the Lord*, her father always said. *Everybody else wants something.*

She took a deep breath. She'd been raised in the hair salon business. Slept in a crib in the office while her mother worked. Sat on her father's shoulders while he made bank deposits. Dealing with people was second nature to her.

Help me learn how to deal with Buck.

Sunny pushed the doorbell and waited.

Nothing. She rapped on the door. When Buck didn't respond, she pounded harder. Suddenly the door swung open and she stumbled against his chest. She looked up at him and gasped.

His long dark hair covered one cheek like a scraggly curtain. The hair on the other side of his head was buzzed short.

Her jaw dropped. "What did you do?"

Strong hands gripped her arms and settled her on her feet. "Found Donnie's clippers." His proud grin faded. "What? Does it look bad?"

"You look like an extra in a horror film." Sunny grabbed his hand. "Come on." She pulled him through the house to the back porch and plugged in her clippers. She pointed a finger at him. "Do not say one word."

For the first time in all the years she'd known him, Buck listened. He actually sat still and closed his eyes.

Sunny got to work, all five senses focused on the crisis before her. Trimming here, sculpting there, she switched clipper guards with rapid movements, creating the style she envisioned in her mind. Her fingers only paused once over a jagged scar on the side of his neck. Where had that come from? He hadn't had that as a kid. Finally, she turned off the clippers and handed him a mirror.

"Ta-da! From zombie to usher in ten minutes." She studied him and nodded. The short cut emphasized his strong jaw and bright blue eyes. He'd look handsome in the pictures. "Don't be surprised if people think you joined the Marines."

He took the mirror she handed him and ran a hand over his buzzed hair. "Won't do much for the swamp boat clientele."

"Pierce your ear and wear a bandana." She turned away and shoved her supplies into her bag.

"What made you come back?" he asked.

His voice was so low, she almost didn't hear him. What would he say if she told him the truth? "I prayed for patience."

His brow furrowed. "You what?"

Ouch. He didn't physically lean away from her, but it sure felt like he did. She stepped back. "I needed to keep my word. I have a business to run." She snatched up her bag. "Now, if you'll excuse me, there's a room full of senior citizens who'll shoot me on sight if I don't get over to Mountain Mist."

Buck jumped to his feet. "You're going there now?"

"Yes." What was she thinking, mentioning prayer to Buck? She pulled open the screen door and scurried from the back porch into the kitchen.

"Give me a minute. I'm coming with you." He followed her inside the house.

Yeah, right. Sunny scurried across the living room to the front door. If she hurried she could finish her Mountain Mist clients before lunch.

"Sunny!" Buck shouted. He snatched the tote bag from her grasp.

She spun around.

With his buzzed hair and intense expression, he glared at her like a soldier on a mission. "Please," he said, lowering his voice. "Start the car. I'll change while you drive."

She yanked her bag away from him. "Why should I?"

Buck shoved his hands in his pockets, a self-conscious expression on his face. "Your comment about praying for patience. I'd just been thinking I needed patience with Gina, and then you said that. Weird."

The anger drained from her. She opened her mouth to speak, to tell him coincidences like that weren't coincidences at all, but the words didn't come.

"I need to go with you to Mountain Mist." Buck said, his voice solemn. "I think your Mr. Quisenbury might be related to Spike."

Chapter Two

Buck angled his body against the back seat of Sunny's VW bug, barely able to peel his damp black tee shirt over his head without jamming his elbow into the headrest. He yanked on a polo shirt then proceeded to pull off his jeans, half-lying in the back seat to slide them over his legs. "Remind me never to ride in your car again."

"And who invited you along?" Sunny gunned the engine.

He struggled into his khakis, grunting as his shoulder banged the window. "You're an awful driver."

"Don't let Kermit hear you say that," she warned.

Kermit? Did Kermit know about Phil? Buck pulled on his shoes. He shouldn't complain. Sunny hadn't asked a single question when he explained the possible connection between Mr. Quisenbury and his father. She'd simply raced out the door and started the engine.

The bug whizzed around the Mountain Mist

parking lot and slipped into a space. Sunny threw open the door and jumped out. "I hate being late." She took off across the parking lot, tottering on her high-heeled sandals, supply bag slung over her shoulder.

Buck extracted himself from the back seat, buckling his belt as he hustled after her. She'd have a heart attack if she didn't calm down. "Tell them it's my fault."

She threw a glance over her shoulder, her silver hoop earrings bouncing against her cheeks. "You run a business. Would you accept a lame excuse like that?"

She had a point.

He watched as she stopped a few yards from the front door. She straightened her shoulders and closed her eyes, breathing deeply. After a few moments, she opened her eyes, smiled, and strolled to the entrance, as elegant as a runway model.

Impressive. Where did she learn to do that? He slowed his stride and followed her into the lobby.

"Thank goodness you're here!" A massively-pregnant red-haired woman came out from behind the counter. "You don't know cranky until you've got a dozen seniors worried they'll be late for the social event of the season."

Buck froze. Donnie and Leanne's wedding was the social event of the season? Good thing he got his hair cut. He glanced around the bright yellow lobby. Comfortable-looking green armchairs were arranged in clusters around the windows. The faint scent of eucalyptus filled the air-conditioned air. Through the doorway that led to what looked like a lounge area, he saw groups of seniors sitting together and chatting. Others sat alone reading or knitting. White-haired and wrinkled, every one.

He gulped. What had he been thinking, tagging along like this? How could he explain his presence? Just blurt out that he thought he might be related to someone who lived here? He reached for Sunny's arm. "I don't think—"

Sunny stepped forward and hugged the red-haired woman at the front desk. "Thanks for covering for me, Jill. This is Buck Day. He came along to visit with my clients while I cut hair."

Wow, she was smooth. Buck exhaled.

"Nice to meet you." Jill shook his hand. "Better get started."

Jill motioned toward the back hall where at least a dozen elderly folks sat waiting. The men were dressed in dark suits, the women in brightly colored dresses and sparkly jewelry. Some sat in wheelchairs, others had canes and walkers. Buck checked his reflection in a mirror they passed. He looked perfectly calm. Why was his heart beating so fast?

"Hi, everybody. Sorry I'm late." Sunny strode past the group and opened a door to reveal a small styling salon with a bright red barber chair. A waist-high counter ran along the mirrored back wall. Styling supplies were neatly arranged on shelves. "I was assisting members of the bridal party. Speaking of which, this is Buck Day, one of the ushers. He's visiting from New Orleans."

A dozen elderly faces stared at him.

Was there toothpaste on his chin? He attempted a smile, hoping he didn't look as out of place as he felt. "Hi."

One man ambled forward with his cane, head erect despite his stooped shoulders. He presented a piece of paper to Sunny, his gesture formal, as if he were bestowing an honor. "The list."

Sunny accepted it with a gracious nod. "Wonderful. Thank you, Colonel Collins." She handed Buck the paper. "Will you escort in the first two people?"

Escort? Buck scanned the list. His shoulders slumped. No Quisenbury.

"Go on," Sunny urged. "No time to dawdle."

His gaze shot to hers. Her tone was all business but her eyes twinkled. So, Mr. Quisenbury wasn't one of the wedding day clients. Had Sunny known that before they'd left? He sighed. Well, he had forced his way along.

He stepped outside. "Mrs. Carter?"

The petite woman sitting in the first wheelchair raised her hand. "That's me."

"May I?" He pointed at her chair handles.

She smiled and nodded as Buck reached for the handles of her wheelchair and rolled her into the room.

"I love your dress. It matches your eyes." Sunny bent to give Mrs. Carter a hug. "Over here, Buck." Sunny lifted a hinged flap in the counter that revealed a sink at just the right height for a wheelchair.

"Impressive!" Buck admired the design as he positioned Mrs. Carter's chair. "Great carpentry work."

"My dad built it." Sunny's voice sounded a little sad.

Did she miss her parents? He watched as Sunny draped a cloth over Mrs. Carter to protect her outfit and gently reclined the back of the wheelchair. She turned on the water and gave Mrs. Carter a shampoo.

"Ahem." The colonel inclined his head toward the paper in Buck's hand.

Oh! Buck stepped outside. "Mr. Zignetti," he read from the list.

A balding man with a circle of bushy white hair hobbled past Buck with his walker. "Hey, Sunny, how's it going? How's Phil?"

"Hi, Mr. Zignetti. Phil and I stopped dating. I told you that." Sunny finished rinsing Mrs. Carter's hair and wrapped it in a towel.

Buck gave Mr. Zignetti a hand up into the barber chair and cringed. If Sunny was still irritated by his earlier cracks about Phil, she didn't show it. The break-up must not have been too painful if she and Phil were still talking on the phone. He watched, fascinated, as her quick fingers rolled Mrs. Carter's hair with small pink curlers and pinned them in place. He couldn't imagine his own large hands fumbling with something that tiny. Those little pink things would be all over the floor.

Mr. Zignetti lifted his chin as Colonel Collins draped a cloth around his neck. "But you're taking Phil to the wedding."

"Not anymore." Sunny rolled another curler and pinned it in place.

He jerked his thumb at Buck. "You taking this fella?"

Sunny blew out a breath. "No need. Buck is already in the wedding."

"Then why's he here?" He gave Buck a narrow-gazed once-over.

Sunny wheeled Mrs. Carter over to the hair dryer. "I brought Buck to tell stories while I cut hair. He owns a New Orleans swamp boat."

Mr. Zignetti eyed Buck as Colonel Collins reached for his comb. "Wrestle any alligators?"

Buck crossed his arms. "No."

"Kill any rattle snakes?"

"Just the ones I run over with my Jeep."

Sunny lowered the dryer top into place over Mrs. Carter's hair. "He's also got this really wicked scar on the side of his neck. Buck, why don't you tell us how you got that scar after you bring in my next client?" Sunny gazed pointedly at the wall clock.

Right. The wedding. He stepped outside. "Mrs. Skokel." Wait. Mrs. Skokel the lunch lady?

And there she was, her round face aglow with the same warm expression that had greeted him every day in the high school cafeteria. Her eyes widened. "I remember you. How's your sister, Reo?"

"She's doing great, ma'am. She's teaching high school in Carsondale." He wheeled Mrs. Skokel to the spot in front of the sink.

"I heard she eloped with Jack Warfield."

"Not exactly, ma'am. They had a small church wedding in Florida," Buck explained. "Jack's mother was recuperating from a bicycling injury and couldn't travel to Lilac."

"I'm looking forward to seeing your sister and Jack at the wedding." Mrs. Skokel patted Sunny's arm. "Just touch it up with the curling iron and give it a good dose of hair spray like Betty Sue used to do. Is it true you and Phil broke up over a trip to Italy?"

Sunny plugged in the curling iron. "Yes, ma'am."

"But, Sunny. Italy." Mrs. Skokel glanced at Buck and sighed. "I always wanted to see the Baths of Caracalla."

Sunny ran a comb through Mrs. Skokel's hair. "The timing was bad."

"Good decision." Mr. Zignetti nodded his approval. "You have a business to run."

Mrs. Skokel spread her hands. "All the more reason to go."

Wow. Sunny's clients knew everything about her personal life. Her relationship with this Phil guy must have been serious if they'd been planning a European trip. Buck never took anyone along when he hit the road—except for that disastrous trip to Las Vegas with Gina.

Sunny wrapped Mrs. Skokel's gray hair around the curling iron. "Too much going on at the shop."

"If you can't keep up with day-to-day business, how are you going to have the time to renovate the MacPhee place?" Mr. Zignetti pointed a finger at her.

Buck's jaw dropped. "You're renovating the MacPhee place?"

"It's a long-term project. Mom and Dad started working on it before they moved to Florida. I thought Reo would have told you." Sunny glanced at her clients. "Buck is Crystalline MacPhee's great-grandson."

Mr. Zignetti smacked the arm of his chair. "You're Carly Day's boy. Should've seen the resemblance." He crossed his arms. "Why doesn't Buck here own the MacPhee place? The MacPhees were his grandparents."

"The MacPhees sold it off ages ago. My parents bought it from Harlan Howell last year." Sunny fluffed up Mrs. Skokel's hair. "Mom always dreamed of moving the salon into that old Victorian. Her plan was to renovate in time for the town's two-hundred-and-fiftieth anniversary celebration."

Buck started. "Lilac is that old."

Sunny clicked her tongue disapprovingly. "You really didn't pay attention in school, did you?"

He felt his lips tug into a grin. "Hated every minute."

"I'd expect nothing less from a man of adventure." Mr. Zignetti eyed the skin beneath Buck's ear. "How did you get that scar?"

Buck puffed out his chest and turned his head, giving everyone a full view. "Feral hog."

Colonel Collins and Mr. Zignetti exchanged skeptical glances.

Buck shrugged. "Walked into a tree limb."

The men burst out laughing. Mr. Zignetti slapped Buck on the back. "You bring this fella next time, Sunny."

Sunny lowered her lashes and smiled. "I'll see what I can do."

Why was it suddenly so hot? Buck jerked around and stuck his head out the door. "Next."

Buck escorted clients in and out of the room for the next two hours. Sunny even asked him to run out to her car twice for additional supplies. Through it all, Sunny and Colonel Collins worked together with quiet concentration, exchanging pleasantries with their clients as they focused on the job at hand. Like the seasoned members of his swamp boat crew, they worked in unison without a lot of fanfare.

Very professional.

When the last client left, he took up a broom and swept the floor. Out of the corner of his eye, he watched Sunny lean against the counter and cross her arms, her gaze fixed on him. "What?" he asked.

She eyed him up and down. "Will the real Buck Day please stand up?"

He dumped the dustpan into the trash can.

"What's that supposed to mean?"

She tilted her head. "Are you the stinker who accused me of dating men for their money, or the helpful volunteer who escorted seniors to the barber chair? Inquiring minds want to know."

He snorted. "Don't let my customer service act fool you. We get a lot of older passengers on the tour boat."

Sunny narrowed her gaze. "So, deep down you're a stinker?"

"Deep down I'm a loner." He turned away and stared into the lounge, scanning every face. "Mr. Quisenbury's not here, is he?"

"No. I kept an eye out while I was cutting hair. He didn't show up."

He stored away the broom, hoping his disappointment didn't show. "Does he ever come to the lounge and visit with other residents?"

"Sometimes." Sunny lead the way to the lobby, waving to folks as she went. "He's kind of a loner, too."

Was being a loner a genetic trait? "Think he'll be at the wedding?"

"It's possible. Mrs. Skokel told me Leanne invited all the residents."

When they reached the parking lot, Sunny's smooth fingers touched his arm. "All kidding aside, things went smoother because of you. Thanks."

Warmth spread across his skin. He cleared his throat. "Gratitude? I must be doing something wrong."

Sunny opened her mouth to reply just as her phone dinged. She dug it out of her purse. "Gina wants to know what's taking me so long. I'm supposed to be styling the bridesmaids. Are you and Gina okay?"

His jaw muscles tensed. "We're fine."

"You weren't exactly happy with each other yesterday."

He blew out a breath as they hurried to the car. "Gina suddenly didn't want to go to the party after driving ten hours. Yeah, I was annoyed."

"She was still angry with you this morning about Remy."

"Gina was distracting Remy while he worked," he explained. "She could have caused an accident. I had to step in."

"Are you sure it's just a crush?" Sunny asked, extracting the car keys from her bag.

"Remy's a great boat captain. Gina's attention was making things awkward. I can't afford to lose him." He brushed a hand across his buzzed hair, unaccustomed to the bristly length. "Gina turns eighteen later this summer. Our mother got married at eighteen."

"You think Gina wants to marry Remy?" Sunny asked as she opened the trunk.

"Don't know. We're seeing her dad tomorrow. Gina needs to go to college or get a job. Not throw herself at my boat captain."

Sunny looked like she was about to say more, but then shrugged and tossed her supply bag in the trunk. "Teenagers come in the shop a lot," she said finally. "It can take them a while to figure out what they want."

He angled his tall frame into the passenger seat and just barely got the car door shut before Sunny revved the engine.

The car zipped around the corner. "I have to stop at the salon to pick up more supplies," she said.

So, Sunny's work days were long, too. On a typical day at the dock, he'd be up before dawn, making sure the boat was stocked and the crew was ready. Then he'd be greeting the passengers when they arrived, seeing them off on the cruise, and welcoming them when they returned. The rest of his time was filled with booking clients, ordering supplies, and repairing the boat when needed. In the early days, he'd gone along on every cruise. Now that he had a trained crew and a great captain working for him, he preferred managing things from his dockside office.

The car whizzed down Main Street, pulling into a spot near the Up Do. "You run around like this all the time?"

"Like what? I'll just be a minute," Sunny called over her shoulder as she slipped out of the car.

Buck retrieved his discarded clothes from the back seat and rolled them into a ball. He stepped onto the sidewalk.

"Don't you want a ride home?" she asked

"No, thanks. Be a shame to miss the

wedding because I died in a head-on collision.”

“Ha-ha. I am not a bad driver.”

He shrugged. “If you say so.”

“I haven’t been in a single accident. Ask Kermit.” She proudly patted the roof of her car. “No speeding tickets either.”

“Let me guess. You cut Sheriff Dobson’s hair.” Buck chuckled to himself as he left Sunny standing speechless at the curb.

~

“Say cheese,” the photographer called out.

Buck rolled his shoulders. How many more pictures were they going to take? Somebody poked him in the arm. He glanced around.

“Hey!” Chris spoke out of the corner of his mouth, his blue eyes bright with laughter. “Stop yawning. We’ll never get out of here.”

“Sh.” Reo turned around and grinned at Chris, her poufy skirt bouncing against Buck’s tuxedo pants. “My turn to race you to the food table.”

First, there were pictures on the steps of St. Andrew’s Catholic Church before the ceremony. Afterwards, there were pictures on the altar. Now, they were posing for pictures under an arch in the church hall with an overflowing buffet within smelling distance. If that wasn’t torture, Buck didn’t know what was. “Bet Jack thanks you every day for having a small wedding,” he whispered to Reo.

Leanne turned around and glared at them.

Buck cleared his throat and attempted to look cheerful. Processions, flowers, solos.

Would the production never end? The only thing that had kept him awake during the ceremony was thinking about his visit to Mountain Mist with Sunny and the idea that the man who held the key to half his family tree might be at the wedding. From his seat at the side of the altar, he'd studied every elderly male face during the ceremony, frustrated he didn't know exactly what kind of physical features he was looking for. Was he tall or short? Broad or thin? Bald or white-haired?

"Back row, two steps right," the photographer called out.

Sunny approached the arch. Wearing a pale lime green dress that floated around her like butterfly wings, she'd positioned herself at the photographer's side, flitting forward to comb hair and straighten collars before each picture was snapped.

She tapped Buck's arm, her flowery scent tickling his senses. "Ew, what's that smudge on your face?"

Smudge? Buck ran a hand down his jaw.

"Kidding." Sunny pulled him two steps to the right.

"Is he here?" Buck whispered.

Sunny shook her head, her face inches from his as she brushed the lapels of his black tuxedo jacket and adjusted his bow tie. Flecks of gold ringed her toffee-brown irises. He'd never noticed that before. She hurried down the steps to her spot beside the photographer.

"Just a few more shots with Donnie and

Leanne," the photographer announced. "Everyone else can go."

As Sunny stepped forward to adjust the train of Leanne's gown, Reo slipped one arm through Jack's and another through Chris'. "Time to raid the hors d'oeuvre table. Come on, Gina." Reo glanced around. "Where'd she go?"

Buck had watched Gina hurry away from the group as soon as the photographer released them, her phone pressed to her ear. "I'll go get her."

After weaving through the crowd shaking hands with people he barely remembered, Buck stepped outside and drew a deep breath, filling his lungs like a man emerging from under water. Marriage. Vows. Till death do us part. He'd watched the ceremony, he'd heard the words. He just didn't know if he could ever believe them. Carly Day and Spike had taken care of that.

During the ceremony, he'd sneaked a look at the enormous cross over the altar and held his breath, not sure what he was waiting for. That odd feeling he'd experienced when Sunny mentioned praying for patience settled over him again. He shifted his shoulders, uncomfortable. He hadn't spent much time thinking about God as an adult. When he was a kid, Donnie and Reo used to drag him off to church every Sunday before he figured out he could get up early and disappear on his bicycle.

His jaw tightened. He didn't need to rely on anyone then, and he didn't need to rely on anyone now. For better or worse, his parents' irresponsible behavior had made him self-sufficient, a successful businessman who'd built his tour boat business from scratch. Sure, he'd had tough times, but he'd learned to be his own person. Gina needed to be her own person, too. She needed to find something she was good at and work at it. Otherwise she'd drift from one thing to another like their mother did.

The setting sun cast a rosy glow along Main Street, making it look like a picture-postcard small town with a proud history and deep roots. He took a deep breath. If there was one thing Gina needed, it was roots. Just because Lilac had never worked for him didn't mean it wouldn't work for her. Would she consider settling down here? All this drifting between family members had to stop. If he could just convince her of that.

He strolled around back. Gina stood beneath a tree near the edge of the parking lot, thumbs rapidly tapping her cell phone. He approached slowly. "Wanna eat?"

"This is boring." Her voice was distracted. She didn't look at him, just stared at her cell phone as if some magic message was going to appear that would make everything wonderful.

He searched his brain for something that might make her want to come back inside. "Reo and Chris are waiting for us."

"There's nobody here my age."

Buck tugged at his collar, itching to undo the strangling bowtie. "Well, that can happen at events like this." Like he was an expert. He avoided these kinds of receptions like the plague.

"Dev's not here. Why did I have to come?" Gina demanded.

He didn't have an answer for that one. Their half-brother Dev was even more of a loner than Buck. The son of a British historian, Dev had not spent a lot of time with his American siblings. Chris was the only one who seemed to know how to find Dev, and, right now, Dev did not want to be found.

Gina looked up from her phone and glared at him. "I don't want to be here," she cried. "Why don't you understand?" She took off around the far side of the church hall.

Patience. Right.

Buck shoved his hands in his pockets and walked inside. The DJ pumped country music through the loud speakers. Couples swirled around the dance floor, Texas Two-Step style. No surprise, Donnie and Leanne were already dancing since they'd told everyone that a dance contest had brought them together in the first place.

Someone grabbed his arm and pulled him around.

"Buck Day! How's it going, man?" Dewey Deutsch pumped Buck's hand in a vigorous shake. His shirt was drenched with sweat from dancing, his red hair sticking out at all angles. He reminded Buck of a Labrador retriever who'd just emerged from a river, soaking wet and happy.

Buck grinned. "No complaints. Furniture store keeping you busy?"

Dewey swiped his brow with his sleeve. "Not as busy as being a town councilman."

"Congratulations. When'd that happen?" Buck asked. Dewey's father Frank had been on the town council for years.

"Last fall. Won the special election after Sunny dropped out." Dewey winked. "But you probably already know that."

Buck's ears perked up. "Didn't know Sunny was into politics."

Dewey scratched the back of his neck. "Mayor Burgin gave her a temporary appointment last summer to fill an empty council seat."

"She was on the town council?" Buck was stunned. How did she find the time between managing the salon and volunteering at Mountain Mist?

Dewey glanced around. "She ran a good campaign. Dropped out when her dad had the heart attack."

That's why her parents had retired to Florida. Buck scanned the crowd looking for Sunny. Why hadn't she told him about her father's health?

"Watch out for this guy." Jack joined them, pointing his thumb at Dewey. "He'll have you joining the bowling league faster than you can say strike."

Dewey's face lit up as he shook Jack's hand.

"Congratulations! Boy or girl?"

Buck's head jerked around. He stared open-mouthed at his brother-in-law. "You're kidding."

"Sorry." Jack punched Dewey in the arm. "Way to spoil the surprise, man."

Dewey shrugged. "Lulu told me."

"The Shoebox Diner waitress knows my sister is pregnant before I do?" Buck shook his head. Was nothing private anymore?

Dewey spread his hands. "Dude, it's Lilac."

~

"I'm worried about Gina." Reo carried a plate heaped with grilled asparagus tips to the back of the hall, away from the crowded dance floor.

Sunny nodded. "She seems kind of lost."

The reception hall was crammed full with tables for both sitting and standing to accommodate all the guests. Reo found an empty standing table and set down her plate. "That's the word."

"Didn't she live with you and Jack for a while?" Sunny asked, taking a sip of iced tea.

Reo bit a stalk of grilled asparagus and swallowed. "On and off. When her stepmother would ask her to babysit too much, she'd come live with us. I made her complete her homework before she could go out with her friends. When she got tired of that, she moved back to her Dad's house. It helped being able to see her every day at school. Now that she's graduated, I'm not sure what's going to happen."

Sunny watched Reo's eyes get big as she stared at something over Sunny's shoulder.

"You were going to tell me when?" Buck hovered over them, hands on his hips, glaring at his sister. Before Reo could reply, he pulled her into a hug. "Congratulations!"

"I'm so sorry I couldn't tell you in person," Reo wailed.

"It's my fault," Sunny blurted. "Someone must've overheard me last night when I guessed."

"Guessed?" Buck eyed his sister up and down. "Based on what?"

Reo rolled her eyes. "Sunny's been surrounded by women since before she could walk. If she can't spot a pregnant female, nobody can."

Sunny polished her fingernails on her dress. "One of my many super powers."

Buck arched an eyebrow at her. "Like discovering lost family members?"

Sunny's face suddenly felt warm. It didn't help that Buck looked like he'd stepped out of a tuxedo store advertisement. She'd hardly been able to keep her eyes off him.

"Who? Gina?" Reo's curious gaze darted between them.

Buck gave Sunny a surprised look then turned to his sister. "There's an elderly resident at Mountain Mist whose last name is Quisenbury."

"Quisenbury? Oh, Quisenbury!" Reo clutched Buck's arm. "Is he related to Spike?"

"I don't know. Sunny took me to Mountain Mist today and—Hi, Leanne."

Sunny jumped at Buck's unnaturally bright tone. She whirled around.

Leanne approached and kissed Reo on the cheek, her smile stiff, like one of those painted Mardi Gras masks. "Congratulations! I just heard the wonderful news. You and Jack must be so happy." She wagged a finger at Reo. "I'm a little disappointed you didn't tell Donnie and me first."

Reo opened her lips as if to respond, but Leanne had already turned to Sunny, her smile pulled tight across her bright white teeth. "Sunny, would you come to the bridal lounge with me, please?"

"Sure." Sunny heard Buck chuckling as she followed Leanne out of the reception hall to the small changing room. Shoes and hangers littered the carpet, open luggage covered the small sofa. The bride's going away outfit hung on a hook.

Leanne shut the door and whirled around. Both manicured index fingers pointed at her head. "What is this?"

Sunny gulped. "What is what?"

"This bump." Leanne touched a specific spot on the side of her up do. "I saw it when I took off my veil."

Sunny leaned close and squinted. "I don't see a bump."

"Don't see a bump? It's gigantic." Leanne turned and stared into the mirror. "How can you not see it? My entire head looks lopsided."

The customer's always right except when she's not, her mom used to say. "You look wonderful," Sunny gushed.

Leanne scowled and handed Sunny a hairbrush. "You have to fix it."

Sweat trickled down Sunny's back. Leanne could end up having a whole lot more than a little bump if Sunny attempted to fix her hair here. It could be a total disaster. *Okay, God, I really need your help now.*

The door opened. Gina walked in, her expression pained. "Could you give me a ride home?"

Leanne crossed her arms. "I assume you're talking to Sunny, and, no, she cannot. She has to fix my hair."

Gina's gaze dropped to the floor like a scolded puppy.

Couldn't Leanne see something was bothering Gina? Sunny put her arm around Gina's slender shoulders. "What's the matter? Don't you feel well?"

Gina shrugged. "I'm tired."

It didn't take a rocket scientist to see the boredom etched on the teenager's face. Sunny smiled. "Tell you what. If you bring me my supply bag from my trunk, you can take my car and drive yourself home. It's the green VW bug in the back corner of the lot."

Gina's face brightened. "I'll be right back." She took the keys from Sunny and hurried out of the room, puffy skirt bouncing.

Leanne looked skyward. "I suppose it's too

much to expect good manners."

Sunny stiffened. "Are you talking about Gina?"

"I've never seen a young person more in need of guidance and more determined not to accept it," Leanne said, her tone firm.

"You're family now. You could help her," Sunny sputtered.

"I'm Reo's stepmother." Leanne patted her hair. "The rest of her half-siblings are extended family."

How could Leanne be so hard-hearted? Sunny lifted her chin. "That's not how Donnie feels. He raised Buck after Carly Day left."

"That may be," Leanne replied, staring at the mirror. "But Donnie never adopted him."

Never adopted Buck? A wave of sadness washed over her. She'd always assumed that Donnie had adopted Buck. No wonder Buck had reacted to her news about Mr. Quisenbury the way he had. He could be a living link to Buck's real father.

"Now, don't go thinking I'm the evil stepmother. I like them all well enough." Leanne brushed a fleck from her bodice. "I just don't want any of them moving in with Donnie and me now that we're married."

Sunny pasted on her sweetest smile. "I don't think you have anything to worry about."

After Gina brought her the supply bag, it took Sunny the better part of twenty minutes to repair Leanne's hairstyle. With Leanne finally satisfied, Sunny returned to the reception. She scanned the crowd. The DJ had turned up the music. The celebration was in full swing. She needed to find Reo and ask for a ride home at the end of the night. She felt a tap on her shoulder and turned around.

"Sunny, a word?" Jim Dobson, Lilac's off-duty sheriff, shouted over the music.

Sunny followed him into the hallway outside the reception.

He cleared his throat and leaned down. "Did you lend your car to Buck's sister, Gina?"

"Yes." Sunny's breath caught at the sound of Jim's serious tone. "What's wrong?"

He glanced around as if to make sure no one was in earshot. "She had a tire blowout on Interstate 81. Scraped the side of your car along the guard rail."

Sunny gripped his arm. "Is she hurt?"

"Scared, but okay."

Relief shot through her. "Where is she?"

"At the station. My deputy just called me. She doesn't want to come back here."

Sunny looked at the crowded dance floor. "I'll go get—"

Sheriff Dobson shook his head. "She doesn't want anyone to make a scene at the reception. She asked for you."

"Someone from her family has to come." Sunny nibbled her lip. "She lives with Buck. I'll get him. We'll come over to the station."

Sunny wove through the crowd and found Buck talking with Dewey Deutsch. "Mind if I steal Buck away?"

Dewey's gaze moved back and forth between them. "If you tell me when you two started dating."

Sunny froze. "We're not dating."

Dewey winked at her. "You're a wild one, Sunny."

Buck frowned, his expression stiffening. "What are you talking about?"

Dewey leaned close to Buck and nudged him in the side. "Heard about you climbing out of Sunny's car at Mountain Mist. Buckling your belt."

Sunny watched in horror as Buck clenched his hand into a fist. She linked her arm in his and yanked him towards her. "Dewey Deutch, how dare you imply such a thing? Buck was changing clothes in my back seat because we were late for an appointment." She shook her finger under Dewey's nose, making sure her voice was loud enough to be heard by the guests standing nearby. "I'll forgive you this time, but if I ever hear you say something like that again, I'll give my clients the name of your discount furniture supplier so they can buy direct and save your thirty-percent markup."

Dewey's mouth fell open as she spun on her heel, pulling Buck with her.

Buck stared at her, dumbfounded. "You just defended my honor."

"Somebody had to. In Lilac, a rumor like that can take a lifetime to erase."

His brow crinkled. "I owe you, I think."

Sunny pulled him towards the entrance.

"Remember that when we're at the police station."

Chapter Three

Buck sat on the edge of Sheriff Dobson's desk, arms crossed as he studied his sister. She huddled on the wooden bench in the circle of Sunny's arms, her eyes swollen from crying, her shoulders shaking with each sob.

He glanced around. How many times had Donnie come here to fetch him? Same old octagonal metal clock ticking away on the wall. Same old oak desk with the chipped corner. Buck had sat on that very bench the last time he'd run away. Old Sheriff Pettibone had brought him back and made him swear not to do it again. In exchange, the sheriff had promised to tell him any information he learned about Carly Day or Spike.

The last time he'd run off was to find out if the rumor eight-year-old Sunny had told him was true. That his mother had married again and given birth to a baby girl.

The same girl who now sat crying on the bench.

He gripped the edge of the desk. "What the heck were you thinking?"

She didn't answer. Wouldn't even look at him.

He struggled to keep the anger out of his voice. "You could've been killed."

Her sobbing increased.

This was not the way he'd imagined this evening would end. He'd been hanging on the edge of the crowd, talking with the men, when Sunny approached, her intense gaze locked on him like a laser. For one crazy second, he'd thought she was going to ask him to dance. His reaction had stunned him: he'd wanted her to.

He blew out a breath. Right now, Sunny was probably wishing she'd had nothing to do with him or his family. He cringed, remembering how she'd patted the roof of her lime green VW, Kermit, proud about no tickets and no accidents.

Now, the side of her car was dented and scratched because of Gina.

He studied Sunny as she comforted Gina, her head bent, murmuring softly. If Sunny was mad, she wasn't showing it. He tried again. "Why were you out on the highway? It takes five minutes to drive to Donnie's house from the church."

"I just wanted to go for a ride," she said between sniffles, her voice choked.

Sunny gently brushed the hair out of Gina's eyes. "Were you going back to New Orleans?"

Gina's head popped up, eyes wide. She didn't say anything.

Sunny reached for her hand. "Do you miss Remy?"

Gina nodded.

Buck jumped to his feet. "I told you he's—"

Sunny's warning glance strangled the words in his throat. He sat down.

"Tell me about Remy," Sunny encouraged with a gentle smile.

Gina sniffed, hesitating. "He's really nice. He listens." She shot a look at Buck. "And he's really cute. He's got an earring and this awesome tattoo on his arm that looks like a sea serpent."

"Cool." Sunny nodded. "Would Remy want you driving so far by yourself at night?"

Gina stiffened. She shook her head.

Sunny squeezed Gina's shoulders. "Neither would Buck."

Gina broke down sobbing and collapsed into the circle of Sunny's arms. "I'm sorry I wrecked your car."

"Sh. It's okay." Sunny stroked Gina's back, her gaze focused on Buck.

He gulped. All the anger drained out of him as he watched his sister melt into the warmth of Sunny's forgiveness.

So, that's what mothers did. He shifted his shoulders, his tuxedo jacket suddenly too tight.

When Gina left to splash water on her face, Sunny's shoulders sagged. "I'm sorry. If I hadn't loaned Gina my car, none of this would've happened."

He crossed the room and dropped into an empty chair beside her. "It's not your fault. I took on more than I could handle when I invited

Gina to live with me." He rested his elbows on his knees and stared at the floor. "Thought I was helping, but I see now I've done more harm than good."

~

Sunny's senses went on high alert. In the salon, when a client said she'd done more harm than good, it was always followed by a terrible story. She gulped. "What do you mean?"

"Last summer, Reo discovered our grandmother grew up here in Lilac. Neither of us knew." Buck blew out a breath. "I wanted to learn what other family secrets Carly Day was keeping. Gina begged to come with me to Vegas last weekend. She hadn't seen our mother in almost ten years. I said no, but she kept asking. She can be very persistent."

She nodded, remembering how insistent Gina had been about jumping out of Buck's car the day before.

"Carly Day was dealing blackjack. I showed up alone and surprised her. She recognized me but didn't say anything. I struck up a conversation with another player, asked if he could recommend a good restaurant nearby since I was staying upstairs. That evening, Carly Day called our hotel suite and asked if I wanted to meet her for dinner." He smiled sadly and shook his head. "Gina was so excited."

"I imagine she was. What happened?"

The muscle jumped in Buck's jaw. "Carly Day seemed happy to see us, shocked by how much Gina had grown. She and Gina cried and hugged. Very touching—until Carly Day asked us to tell everyone she was our aunt, not our mother." He stared straight ahead, hands gripping his knees. "I never should've taken Gina to Vegas."

She tried to imagine Buck dealing with his sister's heartbreak. Her heart sank. "You meant well."

A wry smile touched his lips. "So did you, when you loaned Gina your car." He stared out the window. "Gina's impulsive. She even wanted to drop out of high school, just like our mother." He shook his head. "Neither had a stable upbringing like you had."

Sunny's hand flew to her cheek. "Oh, no."

"What?"

She closed her eyes. "I feel awful. I was complaining about my mother's behavior yesterday. Gina must've thought I sounded so ungrateful."

Buck looked surprised. "What's wrong?"

She pressed her lips together and shook her head, disappointed with herself. "I'm supposed to be managing the shop since my parents retired. My mom calls all the time to check up on what I'm doing. I can hardly breathe without her commenting on it. She even knows if I'm running low on a particular styling product."

"How does she find out?" Buck straightened. He sounded intrigued.

"She keeps up with all her Lilac friends. They talk about everything. It's like she never left."

"Sounds like your mother can't delegate. It's a no-win situation if you can't trust your employees."

Trust. She'd always thought of herself as her mother's daughter, not as her employee. Was there a difference?

Buck stretched his back. "Don't worry about Gina's reaction to your comments about your mother. All five of us had to grow out of that."

Her gaze lingered on the circles below his eyes. He looked so tired. "Grow out of what?"

"Envying other people's families." He ran his hand over his short-cropped hair. "I hate giving this town more gossip about mine."

He sounded so resigned. She wished she could ease his disappointment. "If it's any consolation, the gossip was not about you."

"Right. I'm sure nobody said a thing all those times I ran away." He untied his bow tie and loosened the top button of his white tuxedo shirt. "Tomorrow Gina can sit down with her father and decide what to do next." He leaned back and closed his eyes.

Her gazed rested on the sharp planes of Buck's face, his full lips drawn tight. She folded her hands in her lap, fighting the urge to comfort him. The loner she'd known her entire life would not appreciate it.

"Um," a small voice said behind them.

Sunny looked over her shoulder. Gina stood in the doorway, a guilty expression on her face.

"About my Dad." Gina stared at the floor.

Buck slowly rose to his feet. "Yes?"

Gina gripped the door frame, her knuckles whitening. "He went back to Mexico."

Sunny closed her eyes, waiting for the explosion.

Miraculously, Buck kept his tone low. "Why?"

"Maria's not a U.S. citizen." The words exploded from Gina's lips. "Dad told everyone they're married, but they're not. They were afraid she'd get deported."

Buck rubbed his hand over his face. "How long ago did this happen?"

Gina didn't say anything.

"Gina." He said her name so softly Sunny almost didn't hear him.

"I want to go back to New Orleans!" Gina cried. "I thought if we went to Dad's house and he wasn't there, you'd have to take me with you. But now you think there's somebody in Lilac who might be related to Spike. I heard you two talking this morning." She clenched her hands at her sides. "You ran off to Mountain Mist with Sunny and forgot about me. You were supposed to take me to Leanne's to get ready for the wedding. I had to walk."

Buck took a deep breath and blew it out. "Gina, I'm sorry I didn't take you to Leanne's. But that doesn't excuse you keeping your Dad's move to Mexico a secret, or putting a dent in Sunny's car. Who knows how much that repair is going to cost? You realize, you're going to have to pay for it."

Sunny's heart squeezed at the look of alarm

on Gina's face. If someone had told her at seventeen she'd have to pay to fix a car she'd damaged, she'd have been frantic.

Buck walked to the door, his expression resigned. "Let's go."

They filed out of the sheriff's office and climbed into Buck's sports car. Dark clouds had moved in, casting blotchy shadows over the full moon. They rode in silence with the windows open, the mountain air chilling Sunny's shoulders. A few cars lingered in the church parking lot, most likely the cleanup crew readying the hall for Sunday activities. Sunny nibbled her bottom lip. Leanne hadn't liked it when Gina said she wanted to leave the reception. Had Donnie been disappointed when he noticed Buck and Gina were missing at the end of the night? Sunny cringed. This was all her fault.

As Buck pulled into her driveway, automatic sensor lights came on, brightening the exterior of the house. Buck nodded his approval. "We have lights like these at the dock."

"My dad installed an updated security system here and at the shop before they moved to Florida."

"Can't be too careful. Even in a small town." Buck walked Sunny to the front door, hands shoved into his pockets, white shirt glowing in the porch light. "I'd like to come over tomorrow after lunch, talk about the car, if that's okay." His words sounded tight from strain.

"Sure." Sunny nibbled her bottom lip. "Don't be mad at Gina. My car can be fixed."

He glanced over his shoulder to where Gina sat waiting in the back seat. He blew out a breath. "There's more at stake than a car repair."

"I know." The concern in his voice tugged at Sunny's heart. Gina was at a crossroads. If Buck took the wrong approach, it could push Gina to rebel, send her careening down a self-destructive path.

He gripped the porch rail, his expression tense. "Thanks for not freaking out."

Her gaze locked with his, drawn into the watchful blue depths. Freak out. That's exactly what some of her clients would have done. And spread gossip all over town. Sunny had no plans to do either.

"No worries." She gave him a reassuring smile.

With a silent nod, he pushed off from the railing and followed the beam of light across the lawn. A moment later she heard the soft purr of the engine as he drove away.

She wished she could do something to relieve the sadness in his face. "Help them," she whispered, as a ray of moonlight broke through the clouds.

The security system turned on the interior lights as soon as Sunny entered the house. She kicked off her shoes and headed up the stairs. Buck was self-reliant, a private man who kept his problems to himself. Today, he'd let down his guard, sharing his hope and his fear. Hope he'd discover more about Spike. Fear he'd provide the wrong guidance to Gina.

Sunny passed the framed family portrait as she climbed the staircase to her bedroom. Her dad's dependable smile, her mom's proud expression, and eighteen-year-old Sunny in her high school graduation gown, nestled in between.

This is not your problem, her mom's standard reply whenever Sunny relayed some heart-breaking story she'd heard from a client. *Do not get involved.*

But Sunny was already involved, in more ways than she wanted to admit.

~

"What'll it be, Buck?" Lulu asked over the chatty voices of the Sunday morning crowd.

Buck perused the menu. Not that he needed to. The majority of dishes served at the Shoebox Diner hadn't changed since before he was born.

Lulu filled his coffee cup. "You might like the Sunday special after the night you had."

No surprise, Lulu had already heard all about it. "Sounds good." He forced a smile and handed Lulu the menu, his gaze moving to the scene outside the window. Across the street, the big red doors of the St. Andrew's Catholic Church opened wide.

He did a double-take as the priest emerged. Donnie and Leanne's marriage ceremony had been performed by Leanne's great uncle, a white-bearded monk wearing a simple brown robe who'd looked older than Santa Claus. This priest looked like he could play professional football. Over six feet tall, he stood among the congregation, smiling and shaking hands.

He thought suddenly of his first trip to New Orleans. He'd seen some terrible storm footage online and impulsively quit his construction job in Richmond to go down and help rebuild. He'd been assigned to work on an elementary school and had set up his campsite near the other volunteers. One morning, he'd awoken to the sound of singing. He'd never heard the peaceful hymn before, and yet the words sounded familiar. Chin propped on his fists, he'd lain on his stomach and watched. The group of volunteers were assembled around a picnic table that held two candles and a cross. A Catholic priest stood before them, saying mass.

"Here you go," Lulu placed a steaming plate of food on the table. "Let me know if you need anything else."

He nodded, his stomach growling as he inhaled the aroma of bacon and fresh biscuits. "Thanks."

Just as he was lifting a forkful of food to his mouth, he spotted Sunny exiting the church. Bright as a sunflower in her yellow dress, she talked and laughed with the folks gathered on the sidewalk. Two small children hurled themselves at her legs, hugging Sunny tight as she laughed and hugged them back.

At least, she's smiling. That was a good thing. Buck watched as she finished speaking with the surrounding adults and walked away.

He was amazed at how calm she'd been last night. No angry words. No angry looks. She'd seemed more concerned about Gina's welfare than the damage to her car.

And he'd insinuated she was dating that Phil guy for his money. What an idiot!

He pulled out his phone and reviewed his messages. The shipment of paper supplies for the refreshment stand arrived. Remy wanted to adjust this week's schedule to accommodate another group. Buck read through each notification and sent his responses. Not only was Remy a great captain, he also had a mind for managing business details. Buck would've been in a total jam if Gina had scared him off with her flirting and carrying on.

By the time he finished eating and walking to his car, the sun had disappeared. Gray clouds hovered over the mountain ridge as he pulled up to Sunny's house. He remained in the driver's seat a moment, watching her. She'd changed out of her dress into jean shorts and a pink tee shirt. Kneeling by the garden, she jabbed a trowel into the soil with quick, precise movements. Then she took a white-and-yellow blossomed plant from a tray and dropped it into the hole and pounded the soil around it. She moved a few inches to the right and jabbed the trowel into the soil again. He shook his head, amazed. Even on her hands and knees in the dirt, she looked happy.

Sunny started at the sound of the car door shutting. She sat back on her heels and shook her hair out of her face. She wore dirt-caked work gloves, much too large for the delicate hands that had cut his hair the day before.

He crossed the lawn in a few strides. "I could hear the soil screaming all the way to the curb."

She squinted up at him. "What?"

"You. Jabbing at the dirt." He mimicked her digging motion with his hand. "Looked like you were teaching it a lesson."

"Ha ha." She stripped off her gloves and tossed them onto the grass. "Guess I'm frustrated. I meant to have these daisies in the ground last week. We always plant them in the spring."

"We? I thought your parents were gone." He extended his hand and pulled her to her feet.

Her cheeks reddened. "They are."

He surveyed the yard. "You take care of all this yourself?"

"Try to. Want some lemonade?"

He followed her across the lawn, searching his memory for the last time he'd been here. He'd ditched a boatload of childhood memories when he'd left, determined to get as far away as possible from the small town and its gossiping residents.

"How's Gina?" Sunny asked.

The scent of lilac tickled his nose as Sunny led him up the porch steps. "She was talking with her dad on the phone when I left. Not much he can do from two thousand miles away. Except invite her to join him."

"Will she go?"

"She has no intention of moving to Mexico." His voice stiffened. "And I have no intention of taking her back to New Orleans."

~

A heart-shaped mirror, trimmed with a pink bow, hung by the kitchen sink. Sunny caught a glimpse of herself in it and rolled her eyes. Damp strands of hair escaped from her ponytail, clinging to her cheeks. Her skin glistened with perspiration, flushed from working in the humidity. And she could thank her mother for the shadows under her eyes. The phone had started ringing at seven a.m., waking her from a deep sleep. Her mom, of course, wanted to hear everything about the wedding. Sunny had mumbled her responses, exhausted from the late night, and promised to talk later.

She blew her hair out of her eyes. Why hadn't she paid attention to the time? She'd been so certain it would only take a few minutes to plant the flowers and then get cleaned up. She hated looking sloppy when company came over.

It was just Buck. The guy who'd tied her to a tree when she was eight. They were going to talk about her car. It wasn't like he hadn't seen her covered in dirt before.

She took a deep breath and carried the tray of drinks to the front porch.

Buck sat in one of the wicker chairs, staring straight ahead. "Whatever happened to that noisy German Shepherd that lived across the street?"

"Smokey? He died years ago." She set the tray on the table just as her phone rang. She glanced at the screen and pressed her lips together.

Buck reached for a drink. "Take the call if you need to. I'm not in a hurry."

She tapped the screen and raised the phone to her ear. "Hi, Mom."

"Oh, my God, we just heard about your car. Why didn't you tell me when I called this morning?" Betty Sue's voice vibrated with panic.

"It's just a flat tire and a few scratches. Pete Warfield's gonna fix it." Sunny hoped she sounded reassuring.

"Do you need your father and me to come back and help?" her mother asked anxiously.

"No, it's fine." Why did her mother think she couldn't handle it? "You'll be happy to hear I've got half the daisies planted."

Betty Sue ignored Sunny's attempt to change the subject. "How could you have let that girl drive your car?"

"Um." Her gaze shot to Buck.

"What were you thinking?" Betty Sue demanded.

"Gotta go. I'll call you later." She turned off her phone and attempted a laugh, only it sounded more like a choked sob. "She only calls three or four times a day."

Buck didn't smile at her lame joke. "So, it's more than just micromanaging how you run the shop."

She opened her mouth to respond then closed it. Her mom's appetite for every detail about life in Lilac was embarrassing. She shrugged. "She means well."

"Don't have much experience with doting mothers." Buck leaned forward, elbows on his knees, his brow furrowed. "Found out this morning Gina spent every one of her refreshment stand paychecks. I should've set up a bank account for her, taught her about saving."

"Don't blame yourself. You gave her a home and a job."

"The point is she doesn't have money. It's important for her to pay for the repairs. Reo and I talked last night. Making Gina pay you back could help her learn about being accountable."

She hated seeing the lines of worry in his face. The Buck who'd teased her about skinny dipping and joked with the senior citizens was gone, replaced by a serious man concerned about his sister.

Thunder rumbled in the distance. The first spatter of rain drops hit the sidewalk and transformed abruptly into a downpour. So much for getting those daisies into the ground. Plus, she still had the hedges to trim and the sidewalk to edge.

She straightened. "Hey, I've got it. How about if Gina comes to work for me?"

"At the shop?"

"Sure. And here, too." It made perfect sense. "I'll pay her the standard part-time rate we use at the salon. Pete told me this morning the car repairs will only be a couple hundred."

"You're sure?" Concern etched Buck's features.

"If she's okay with doing yard work and shampooing hair." Sunny shrugged. "We can try it out."

"Not sure she's going to like it. But she needs to earn some money." Buck drew his car key from his pocket and held it out to her. "Take mine until yours gets fixed."

"You have to drive back to New Orleans," she protested.

Buck shook his head, his expression resolute. "Not until your car is fixed."

She looked at the key dangling from his fingers. "What about your business?"

"Remy and the crew run the day-to-day operations. I can manage accounts and scheduling from here, at least, for a while." Buck's fingers closed around hers as he pressed the key to her palm. "There's no reason for you to refuse."

"Well," she tried to ignore the tingle of warmth where his fingers touched hers. "Let me help you find out about Norbert Quisenbury. I can ask some of the Mountain Mist residents. Get details about his family."

"No." Buck's expression hardened. "I don't want him feeling like somebody's checking up on him. Who's the Mountain Mist director?"

"Dr. Yasmin Dalir. She's wonderful."

"Good. I'll call her." Buck drained his glass of lemonade and set it on the table. "Would you be willing to come along to the appointment? I might need you to use some of your magic powers and vouch for me." His lips pulled into a wry smile.

He wanted her to be with him when he found out about Mr. Quisenbury. She didn't know why the idea made her so happy. "Sure. Let me know when."

"I will. Thanks." He set down his glass and strode down the steps into the rain.

She jumped to her feet. "You're getting soaked. Don't you want me to drive you home?"

He turned and spread his hands, his clothes plastered to his body. "This is nothing. I live in the swamp."

"But." Her protest died in her throat as he turned and walked away.

Chapter Four

"Do you think it's wise, driving around Lilac in that expensive sports car?" Betty Sue DeStefano's voice rang out over the phone speaker Tuesday morning.

Sunny dusted the Up Do product shelves. She'd wondered how long it would take before someone told her mom she was driving Buck's car. Three days. The Lilac gossip mill was falling down on the job. "I'm just using it until Kermit is fixed."

"I still don't understand why you loaned your car to Gina in the first place," Betty Sue huffed. "Even your father was shocked, and you know he always takes your side."

Please, help me keep calm. Sunny peeled off her rubber gloves and stored them with the cleaning supplies in the storage closet. "The important thing is, Gina is fine and my car is being fixed."

The shop chimes jingled and Sunny's second cousin on her Mom's side, Nadine Johnson, hurried in. "Sorry I'm late. The sitter's sick. I had to drop off the twins with Ms.

Gallagher."

Sunny whirled around, motioning with her hands for Nadine to stop talking.

"Make sure you enter your actual starting time on your timesheet, Nadine," Betty Sue instructed over the speaker, her voice stern.

Nadine's wide-eyed glance flew to Sunny's face.

"Sorry," Sunny mouthed.

Nadine set down her purse, closed her eyes for a moment, and then opened them. "I'll be sure to do that, Betty Sue."

"Sunny," Betty Sue said, her voice still stern. "Lavinia told me you still haven't turned in the list of salon promotions for the Lilac anniversary celebration."

"I've been meaning to discuss that with you." Sunny went to the front counter and flipped open her laptop.

"What's there to discuss?" Betty Sue snapped. "I told you what items and services to put on sale."

"I know you did. I thought it would be nice to have reusable tote bags printed," Sunny replied, fingers racing across the keyboard. "I came up with a design using the salon logo. I'll email it to you." She scrolled through her files.

"Please stick with the list I sent you," Betty Sue said. "We don't need the added cost."

"I checked an online printing service. It's not as expensive as you think." Sunny tapped open a web page. Where was that price list? She was just looking at it the other day.

"I have to go. Time for your father's mall walk." Betty Sue hung up.

Sunny threw her arms wide. "Why doesn't she listen to me?"

Nadine raised her hand. "Do not say another word."

Oh, she had another word to say, all right. "Why not?"

"You're the manager. Betty Sue's the owner. Which means I don't want to be in the middle." She sat next to Sunny. "Do you know Betty Sue called me yesterday to say I cut Helen Watson's bangs too short? Apparently Helen sent her a selfie with the caption 'Christmas elf for hire'. Your mother may have moved away, but she's still in charge."

Sunny cupped her chin in her hand. "I wish I knew what to do."

"What can you do? As long as she holds the purse strings, she's in control."

What about her personal life? Telling Sunny what to do around the shop was one thing. Getting involved in Sunny's personal decisions—like who she chose to loan her car to—was something else.

"Does she know you're going to let Gina start working here?" Nadine asked.

Sunny shook her head.

"Sunny!"

"I'd planned to tell her this morning," Sunny replied, wishing her tone didn't sound so defensive. "I would have if she hadn't gone off about the promotional items."

"Better she hears it from you than somebody else." Nadine walked over to her workstation and set out her supplies for the day.

No kidding. Her mom had made it painfully clear she had not been happy to learn that Sunny was driving around Lilac in Buck's car. When Sunny closed her eyes, she saw Buck walking away from her in the rain, alone. On Sunday afternoon, she'd had an overwhelming urge to reach out to him, to break through the wall he'd built around himself. Whenever she got close enough to see a glimpse of the real Buck, the barrier sprang up again.

Was she selfish for wanting to help? She'd like to think she would help anyone who asked for her assistance. But she knew there was more to it when it came to Buck. Emotions were involved. Feelings she'd stuffed away when Buck left Lilac.

Sunny sighed. If she didn't tell her mom about the working arrangement with Gina, it was only a matter of time before someone else in town spilled the beans. Buck had been right when he'd said her mother was a micromanager. Her mom concerned herself with every detail of Sunny's life, giving her opinion whether Sunny wanted it or not.

And Sunny didn't know what to do about it.

Gina arrived at the stroke of ten, and Sunny introduced her to Nadine. There wasn't time to demonstrate the shampooing procedure to Gina, so Sunny put Gina to work polishing all the mirrors just as the first customers arrived.

"Extensions." Tanya Lee sat in Sunny's styling chair an hour later, twirling her chestnut locks in her fingers. "Definitely extensions."

Nadine looked up from the magazine she was reading and gave Sunny a sympathetic smile. Tanya Lee had recently come into a large insurance settlement, making her set for life and able to indulge every whim, as long as she didn't get too extravagant. Every other week she came into the Up Do with a new idea for a hairstyle, and every time Sunny tried to talk her out of it. Either the cut wasn't suited for Tanya's hair type, or the style wouldn't be flattering to her face shape. Tanya inevitably brought a stack of the latest fashion magazines, fixated on the one style that she was convinced would give her the perfect look.

"You realize there's a lot of work involved with extensions," Sunny advised. "You have to use special shampoo. You can't brush them the way you do your regular hair. You might want to talk to somebody who's had them before you decide."

"I've read all about them online." Tanya tapped the fashion magazine photo resting in her lap. "I know they require more work, but I don't care."

Gina stopped sweeping the floor to glance at the open magazine. She studied Tanya's face in the mirror and shook her head. "That style is not good for you. It will make your face look too long." She pointed to a poster on the wall above the styling station. "Now that cut would look good on you. It would bring out your eyes."

Tanya's gaze moved from the magazine to the poster and settled on Gina's side braid. Dressed in a short denim skirt with a fringed suede top pulled tight with a wide alligator belt, Gina's youthful style was unique and fun.

Sunny held her breath as she and Nadine exchanged worried glances. Neither of them had ever been that direct with Tanya before.

Tanya eyed Gina's gladiator sandals. "Where did you find those?"

Gina grinned. "At a thrift store in New Orleans."

Tanya nodded. "That's what we need around here. You have to drive all the way into Charlottesville to find a decent consignment shop." She pointed at the poster. "Cut it like that."

Sunny couldn't believe it. "No extensions?"

Tanya shook her head. "Gina's right. That cut will bring out my eyes."

When Sunny finished cutting and blew the last locks into place, Tanya looked absolutely stunning. Gina had been right.

Tanya shook her head, her shorter locks swinging around her cheeks. "Wait until Phil sees this." She glanced up at Sunny, her face reddening. "You don't mind, do you, Sunny? Me dating Phil?"

Sunny laughed. "Of course not. We broke up weeks ago."

"That's what Phil said." She smiled. "Plus, I heard you're seeing Buck now."

Crash! Gina knocked over a small trash can with her broom. "Sorry." She bent down and picked it up.

Sunny cleared her throat. "Uh, no. I'm not."

"You're driving his car." Tanya pointed at the sleek black sports car parked in front of the shop.

"He loaned it to me while mine gets repaired." Her face burned.

"Uh-huh." Tanya angled a shrewd smile at Gina. "You'd tell me if Buck and Sunny were dating, wouldn't you, Gina?"

"Assuming they told me," Gina muttered without looking up.

"Of course, we'd tell you," Sunny exclaimed. "But we're not dating, so there's nothing to tell."

Tanya glanced at Buck's car and then at Sunny. "Only a matter of time."

~

The afternoon sun beat down on Buck's back as he knelt beside a bicycle in Donnie's front yard. He checked the tire pressure and screwed the cap on the valve. "Here you go," he called over his shoulder. "It's all ready."

Gina stood in the middle of the driveway, arms crossed. "I am not riding that around Lilac."

Buck rose to his feet and brushed off his jeans. He silently counted to ten before answering. "You said you were tired of walking everywhere so I cleaned up Reo's old bike. It's the perfect size. I even found her helmet."

Gina turned up her nose. "I am not wearing a helmet."

He rolled the bike back and forth a few inches and grinned, hoping she'd get into the spirit. "Come on. It'll be fun."

"Then you ride it." She glanced at her phone. "I have to go."

Buck watched as Gina walked down the driveway and disappeared around the corner. His sister hadn't exactly been thrilled about the deal he'd made for her to work off the cost of Sunny's car repairs. But what choice did she have? She needed to be accountable for her actions. She'd been working for over a week, and he'd hoped to see a change in her mood.

So much for hoping. Gina ate her meals with Buck, but that was about it for spending time together. He tried talking to her about her work with Sunny, but she was always preoccupied with whatever conversation was taking place on her phone.

He wheeled Reo's bike into Donnie's garage, his gaze moving to his old bike in the corner. That one definitely needed work. More than he could do with a cleaning rag and bicycle pump. Still, why not fix it up? He'd explored every corner of Lilac and the surrounding counties on that bike. Especially on those days when he'd overheard another nasty comment about his mother. Whenever that had happened, he'd headed out to the mountains, eager to put as much space as possible between himself and the town gossips.

He ran his hand over the seat, remembering the day Sunny had turned down his invitation to the senior prom. His pickup truck had been out of commission with two blown tires, but that hadn't stopped him from jumping on his bike and escaping. He'd stayed in the hills all night, seeking shelter in the ruin of that old stone church when it had started to rain. He'd sworn that night he was going to leave Lilac and make something of himself.

And he had.

He'd always said he didn't care what everybody thought, but deep down he knew that wasn't exactly true. Even though he preferred driving his beaten up Jeep, he'd bought that expensive sports car for one reason: to flaunt his success. Not that it had been much of a statement. Less than twenty-four hours after arriving in Lilac, his sister had wrecked Sunny's car, giving the town plenty to gossip about.

His phone rang.

"Mr. Day. This is Dr. Yasmin Dalir. Sorry it took me so long to return your call. I was out of town at a conference. Our receptionist indicated you wanted to set up an appointment."

"Yes, I do."

"Do you need to make arrangements for a family member to join us here at Mountain Mist?" she asked.

"Not exactly." How could he explain the situation without sounding crazy? "I believe my father may be related to one of your residents." He told her about Carly Day and Spike, and his suspicion that Mountain Mist resident Norbert Quisenbury may be related to his father.

"Would you like to meet Norbert?"

He hesitated. "I'd like to meet with you first. Discuss how to go about it."

"How about tomorrow, Thursday, at two in my office?" she asked after a moment.

"That would be great. Thanks."

Buck stared at his phone, his heart pounding. This might be it. He might finally learn something about Spike. He'd asked Sunny to come along to the appointment. Did he have a right to drag her into his family business?

~

His question was still unanswered the next day when Sunny drove up to the house. She glided out of his car, wearing a pale pink skirt and silky white blouse with pink polka dots. She strolled to the front porch. "I have a confession to make." Her eyelashes fluttered down then back up as she fixed him with a troubled gaze. "I'm in love with your car."

Buck swallowed a smile and shoved his hands in his pockets. "That bad, huh."

Sunny glanced over her shoulder, her gaze lingering on the vehicle's sleek lines. "I thought I knew what driving was. Then I met Cole."

"Cole?"

"He's given me so much. I thought the least I could do was give him a name." She bit her bottom lip. "You were so right about women loving expensive cars."

His breath hitched. *She's playacting, Stupid.*

"You won't tell Kermit, will you?" She batted her long lashes at him.

Buck rubbed his hand across his mouth, fighting to keep his tone serious. "He won't hear it from me."

The flirtatious expression disappeared and her face broke into a wide grin. "Pete finished this morning. Kermit looks good as new." Sunny extended her hand, the key ring dangling from her fingers. "Take it, before I do something I regret."

Buck shook his head and strode to the passenger side.

Sunny's heels clicked on the pavement as she dashed to the car. "You're letting me drive?"

"Far be it from me to keep a woman from her true love."

Sunny slid into the driver's seat and revved the engine. "You're not jealous?"

Buck slipped on his sunglasses and leaned back. "I'll let you know."

Riding with Sunny in her VW bug was like riding a roller coaster. Sunny at the wheel of a sports car, however, was something else altogether. Smooth. Controlled.

The woman knew how to drive.

"Dad and I used to watch NASCAR together," she confessed as she expertly rounded a curve.

"Ever go to a rally?" he asked as they turned onto the lane leading to Mountain Mist.

"The salon took up all our time. We could

never get away." She held up her hand. "I know. Don't say it. Failure to delegate."

He shrugged. "Just saying. That's how I'm able to manage my business remotely."

"How's that working out?" Sunny asked as she pulled into the Mountain Mist parking lot.

They strolled up the walk. "Fine, so far. Reservations and payments are handled online. Independent contractor stocks the refreshment stand. A local caterer handles special events." He froze at the front door, sweat breaking out on his forehead. "What if we're related?"

Sunny lifted her face to him. All the earlier playfulness was gone, replaced by a sincerity that shone brighter than the afternoon sun. "After doing a million handsprings? I guess you'll deal with it."

You'll deal with it. He certainly hoped so. Right now he felt like he was going to get a root canal. He pulled open the door. Sunny led him across the lobby and down a hall to the administrative offices.

"Come in," Dr. Dalir called through her open door.

Buck stepped into the room and froze. A white-haired man sat with his back to them, facing the desk. Was that Mr. Quisenbury? He thought they were just meeting with the director.

Sunny stepped forward to hug Dr. Dalir. The old man, broad shouldered with a slight stoop, rose slowly to his feet, leaning heavily on his cane. Sunny gave him a kiss on the cheek and then squinted at him. "That eye of yours looks much better. Those drops are doing the trick." She took his arm. "This is Buck, Carly Day's son. You remember Harlan Howell, don't you, Buck?"

The knot in Buck's stomach loosened. He stepped forward and held out his hand. "Sure do. How're you doing, Mr. Howell?"

The old man eyed Buck up and down.

Well, this was awkward. Buck lowered his hand.

"Can't believe he didn't tell me," Harlan muttered. He turned to Dr. Dalir. "Better let Norbert know." He shuffled out of the office.

Dr. Dalir gestured to the empty chairs facing her desk, her expression apologetic. "Why don't you both have a seat?" She walked across the office and closed the door.

Buck shot Sunny a confused glance. "What's going on?" he whispered.

Sunny touched his arm. "It'll be okay," she replied reassuringly, her eyes bright with excitement.

Dr. Dalir sat down and cleared her throat. "Sorry for the theatrics. Because of Norbert Quisenbury's age and health, he thought it would be best to set up this meeting sooner rather than later." She must've noticed the confused look on Buck's face and continued. "Harlan represents Norbert's financial and personal affairs as well as those of many of our residents."

"He's a lawyer," Sunny explained, "and a CPA. They trust him to look out for their interests."

Buck nodded. The news was full of stories about senior citizens being taken advantage of, getting caught in scams and losing all their savings. "How do they know Harlan's trustworthy?"

"Harlan has lived in Lilac forever. His life is an open book." Sunny explained. "In addition to owning a lot of real estate, he's the town archivist. He knows everyone's history."

"He's organized the residents into committees that meet regularly to discuss events concerning the town," Dr. Dalir added. "He makes sure their voices are heard, that they're still contributing members of the community even though they can no longer be as active as they might like."

"What did he mean when he said 'better let Norbert know'?" Buck asked.

"Norbert and Harlan have known each other for ages," Dr. Dalir explained. "Norbert asked Harlan to meet with you first."

"To see if I looked like a Quisenbury?" he asked.

"Yes, I think so." Dr. Dalir stood and stuffed her stethoscope into the pocket of her white medical coat. "I have to make my rounds. Please use my office for as long as you need it." She left, closing the door quietly behind her.

Buck rubbed the back of his neck. Was his fate going to be decided by Harlan Howell, an old man who hadn't seen him in ten years? Buck searched his memory. Had he ever done anything to get on Harlan's bad side? He'd pulled his share of pranks when he was a kid. Went to some of Jack Warfield's wild parties before Jack joined the army and cleaned up his act.

He shifted his shoulders. He felt like he was on trial.

Sunny touched his arm, her expression calm. "Harlan saw what he needed to see. He's a bit of a curmudgeon, but underneath he's a big teddy bear."

Sunny's voice broke through the blood pounding in his ears. He searched her face. "You trust him?"

She nodded. "He helped when I was on the town council last year. He keeps an eye on everything that happens, although he'd deny it if you asked him. Tom Burgin may be the mayor, but Harlan is the heart and soul of Lilac."

"If you say so." If Sunny trusted the old fella, Buck didn't have any choice right now but to trust him, too.

Sunny chuckled. "If I know Harlan, he's already done a background check and knows your credit history, criminal record, and net worth."

"You're kidding."

Sunny shook her head. "Don't be fooled by the cane. My dad says Harlan's brain works faster than a caffeinated jackrabbit."

"How is your dad?" Buck asked, wishing he'd inquired about her father's health earlier. "Reo filled me in on his heart attack. I'm sorry."

"It was scary at first. Now that he's settled in Florida, he seems content. He and Mom walk every day. He eats a special diet. When the doctor said he could resume all his former activities, he started playing golf again."

Buck heard the concern in her voice and touched her hand. "You're still worried about him."

She nodded. "Yes, I'm a daddy's girl. Don't laugh."

"Why would I laugh? Don't you think Reo's a daddy's girl? That's probably why you two get along so well."

Sunny bolted up straight. "I never thought of that."

"Always been obvious to me." His gaze lingered on her delicate fingers, the soft pink polish on her nails. He gulped. "I never thanked you for everything you're doing for Gina."

She smiled. "It's great having Gina at the shop. Pete gave me a good price on the repairs. She's over half-way through the hours she needs to pay me back."

He froze. "You're not just saying that to be nice, are you?"

She cocked her brow at him. "You must have me confused with someone else," she said, her gaze playful.

Warmth shot through him. Nope. Not possible.

The office door banged open.

Harlan gripped the door frame and called into the hallway behind him. "Told you the wheelchair would've been faster."

"Rome wasn't built in a day," an irritated male voice rasped. "Taken a quarter century to meet this grandson of mine. What's a few more minutes?"

Grandson! Buck jumped to his feet, his heart slamming against his chest. He heard the whispering scrape of the walker before he saw the man pushing it. Norbert Quisenbury was bent at the waist, his shoulders hunched as he shuffled into the room. He'd been a tall man once. Now, painfully thin and stooped with age, each step seemed an effort. He wore a crisp white shirt and a dark blue suit, his gray tie flapping with each scrape of the walker. He stopped in the middle of the office and glanced from side to side. With visible effort, the old man straightened and stared directly into Buck's face. Buck stood rigid as the wizened blue eyes studied him.

"Darn, if you don't look just like Norel."

Chapter Five

A group of teenage boys lounged in the Up Do waiting area, laughing and checking their phones. "Gina," the boy with blond hair called out. "How about this?"

Sunny watched as Gina studied the image on the boy's phone, looked at his expectant face, and shook her head. "That cut would not look good on you." She ruffled his wavy blond hair with her hand. "With thick hair like yours, you need something different." She pulled out her own phone and, with a few taps, found a hair style and showed it to him. "What do you think?"

Total adoration shone in his eyes. "Awesome. Can you do it?"

"Sure." Gina jumped to her feet and headed for the styling chair.

"I believe what Gina means," Sunny interrupted, "is that I can do it. Gina hasn't had her professional training yet."

"Oh." The boy's face fell. "Well, can you do it, Sunny?"

Sunny studied the hair style photo on Gina's phone. "Sure. Come on over."

He glanced up shyly. "Don't I get a shampoo?"

She watched his gaze move to Gina. Oh my. Him, too? Ever since Gina had become the shampoo assistant, she was racking up admirers faster than Sunny could cut their hair. "Sure, Gina can take care of that."

Don't I get a shampoo? The same question Buck had asked her on Donnie's back porch a month ago. Back when they were still acting like teenagers, pretending to hate each other to avoid anything resembling a serious conversation.

Gina giggled at something the blond boy said as she lathered his hair.

Sunny sighed. It had been almost two weeks since she'd gone with Buck to meet Norbert Quisenbury. The Fourth of July had come and gone and she hadn't even felt like going to watch the town's annual fireworks display.

From what Gina said, Buck would be staying in Lilac for a while. Sunny had seen him three days ago when she glanced up from her styling station to find his sleek car stopped in front of the shop. He was driving his grandfather down Main Street with the car windows open. Norbert, his gnarled hand raised, was pointing out something in the distance. Both men were smiling. She couldn't blame Buck for spending every free minute with Norbert. Between helping Donnie with house repairs and visiting with his grandfather, Buck clearly didn't have time for anyone else.

She felt a stab of guilt. Buck was getting closer to his family, while she was drifting from hers. She finally had to ask her mother not to call during work hours, since it distracted her from her customers. As a result, Betty Sue had started texting. A lot.

Gina led her customer over to Sunny's chair, a towel draped around his shoulders.

Sunny combed his damp hair, studying the wave of it as it fell. "Gina's right. That cut will look great." She picked up her scissors and got to work. She attempted chatting with her client about his summer vacation and plans for college, but he seemed to prefer being silent. Like Buck.

What had Buck learned about Spike? From Gina's comments, it was clear Buck wasn't saying too much to his sister. Sunny had told herself more than once she had no right to feel hurt that he hadn't thought to share any details with her. He was very private, and she was—she sighed. As much as she might want things to be different, she and Buck were just friends. He'd asked her along to that first meeting at Mountain Mist because she worked there and knew everyone. She had no right to get involved in his personal affairs, even if the touch of his hand on hers had started her entire arm tingling.

Still, what if the family history he'd been learning wasn't all sunshine and roses? What if the facts of his father's life were nothing like he'd imagined? She said a silent prayer, certain that God would not give Buck a burden he couldn't handle.

Sunny made quick work of the cut, her young customer grinning from ear to ear when she finished. She spun his chair around to face the waiting area.

"Hey, Gina. Do you like it?" he called.

Gina sat on the sofa next to another young man, studying haircuts. "Awesome!" she answered, barely looking over her shoulder as she showed the young man next to her what hair style would look best on him.

Sunny watched her customer's face turn red. He reached into his jeans pocket, handed Sunny some money, and stomped out of the shop without another word. Gina didn't even glance up when the door chimes rang and the front door slammed.

Sunny leaned a hip against the counter and crossed her arms. Somebody needed a refresher on hair salon etiquette. "Gina, would you help me a minute in the office, please?"

Gina glanced up. "Sure."

The boy next to her muttered something and Gina giggled.

Sunny shut the office door behind them. "I realize you're new to the salon business, so I want to say a word to you about customer service. We treat all customers equally here."

"I do treat everyone equally." Gina's brow furrowed. "What do you mean?"

"You barely acknowledged our last customer when he left."

Gina spread her hands. "I told him the cut

was awesome."

"He wanted you to look at his hair cut and tell him what you thought," Sunny explained. "Not call out to him over your shoulder."

Gina crossed her arms. "I was working with the next customer."

"It's important to look at customers when you speak to them and answer their questions politely." Sunny's mother must've said that to her a thousand times. "He wanted to hear your opinion."

Gina made a face. "I gave him my opinion. I told him he looked awesome." Her voice sounded frustrated.

Sunny pressed her lips together. How could she explain this? "People remember how you make them feel. How do you think the last customer felt when he left?"

Gina shrugged. "I don't know. I thought you liked me advising people on their hair styles."

"I do like you helping them. But you need to help them *equally*."

"You told me yourself that you didn't have many high school boys coming here for haircuts before I started. Does it bother you I get so much attention?" Gina asked, her tone accusing.

"This is not about getting attention. It's about giving it." Sunny broke off and tried to get her voice under control. Where was this stubbornness coming from? Was this what Buck had meant when he said he sometimes had a hard time reasoning with Gina? "They're customers. It's important to treat each one courteously."

Gina narrowed her gaze. "You're upset about Buck, aren't you? He ignores me now, too."

"We're not talking about Buck," Sunny replied, her jaw tight with exasperation. "We're talking about you."

Gina's bottom lip quivered, her eyes glistening with sudden tears. "I can't do anything right." Her defensive expression crumbled as she slumped into a chair.

Sunny felt like they were back at the police station with Gina sobbing in her arms. She gave Gina a gentle smile. "That's not true. You've been awesome. I'm just trying to teach you about professional behavior."

Gina sniffed. "That's what Buck always talked about. He said it wasn't professional for me to try to talk with Remy when he was working. Do you think that's why Remy hasn't answered my text messages?"

"I don't know." Sunny bit her bottom lip. Maybe Buck hadn't been exaggerating when he said Gina had been distracting Remy. "Sometimes it's important to keep your job separate from your personal life."

"But you've worked here with your family your whole life," Gina said.

Sunny laughed. "It's not like I had a choice." She froze at the sound of her own joke. Was that true? She gazed around the office. Did she have a choice?

Gina took a tissue from the box. "I don't

know what I'm going to do once I finish my hours here." She blew her nose and hiccupped.

"You've got your family. Reo and Buck. Everyone will help you figure it out." Sunny said the words as much for herself as for Gina. "Let's get back to work."

Gina touched her arm. "You won't tell Buck at dinner tonight, will you?"

Sunny's heartbeat skipped with a little jolt. Leanne had called last week to invite Sunny over to eat and see the wedding pictures. She hadn't said anything about Buck and Gina being there. "My lips are sealed."

After the last client left, they turned off the equipment and locked up. Kermit waited for them at the curb, sparkling in the sun. Pete Warfield had done such a good job with the repair, she couldn't even tell there had been any damage.

Gina dragged her feet as she followed Sunny to the car, her face cast downward.

Was Gina still moping about Sunny correcting her? Sunny handed Gina the car keys. "You drive."

Gina immediately perked up. "Me?"

"Unless you don't want to."

"Are you kidding?" Gina took the keys, her expression suddenly bright and eager.

Sunny smiled at Gina's reaction and settled into the passenger seat, excited by the thought of seeing Buck. Don't get ahead of yourself. She could imagine her mother's voice saying that to clients who were anxious about some upcoming event in their lives. Sunny tried to imagine telling her mother about the feelings Buck stirred in her and sighed. Her mother would tell her to stop wasting her thoughts on a loner who didn't know the meaning of commitment.

Gina turned onto Donnie's street.

"I thought we were eating at Leanne's townhouse." Sunny noticed Buck's sports car parked in Donnie's driveway.

"Too many steps to climb at Leanne's. Buck wanted Norbert to come, so now we're eating at Donnie's." Gina pressed the car key into Sunny's hand. "Thanks for letting me drive."

Buck appeared in the doorway wearing a navy polo shirt and khakis. He met them on the front walk. "Hey, Gina. Leanne needs your help with a recipe."

"Which one?"

"Something with meat, I hope." Buck spread his hands. "Since when did Leanne decide she and Donnie needed to be vegetarians?"

Gina trotted into the house, laughing.

Buck stood before Sunny, hands shoved into his jeans pockets. "Walk?"

Sunny's smile disappeared at the sight of his serious expression. She nodded and fell into step beside him.

Buck jerked a thumb over his shoulder. "Donnie's showing old photos to Norbert."

Gravel crunched beneath her shoes. "That's a bad thing?"

"Kind of weird. There aren't a lot. Some with you and Reo." His voice trailed off.

She thought of the shelves of photo albums in her house, chronicling every stage of her growth from birth through high school. At her mom's insistence, her father had painstakingly scanned hundreds of their favorite images onto the computer so they could still see the pictures after their move to Florida.

She elbowed his arm playfully. "Cowlicks? Frosting face? You wearing a super hero costume?"

"Maybe." Buck's lips tugged into a brief, embarrassed smile before his tone turned serious again. "Donnie showed pictures of Carly Day and me. I saw the look on Norbert's face. He recognized her."

A sick feeling settled in her stomach. "You think Norbert has known all along you were Spike's son?"

Buck was silent for a long time, his expression closed. "I don't know," he said finally. "All he's told me so far is that Spike is dead."

"I'm so sorry." She threw her arms around Buck's shoulders.

His arms stayed rigidly at his sides.

Embarrassment shot through her like electric current. She released him and stepped back, clearing her throat. "People always have reasons for what they do. Give Norbert a chance to explain." She struggled to steady her voice, while her heart felt like it was breaking. Could the ground just open up and swallow her now?

"The eternal optimist. Another one of your

super powers? Doesn't anything bad ever happen to you?" he challenged, his voice flat.

Her gaze shot to his face. "Your sister wrecked my car."

His shoulders jerked as if she'd smacked him.

She choked back a startled laugh.

Buck shook his head. "Guess I deserved that."

She crossed her arms. "Just because I try to be positive, it doesn't mean I'm happy all the time."

He raked his hand through his hair. "I don't know how you put up with all this emotional drama. Makes me glad I live in the swamp."

They reached the corner and stopped. She schooled her expression, as she'd done so many times before when a salon client said something that filled her heart with sadness. "Doesn't it get lonely?" she asked finally.

"Solitude suits me just fine," Buck replied as they turned and headed back.

~

Bright morning sunlight glinted off the polished hood of Buck's car. He shot a sideways glance at his grandfather. "Mind telling me where we're going?"

Norbert stared straight ahead at the rolling green hills spread around them. "You'll see."

Aside from Buck's observation that Norbert already knew who Carly Day was, dinner the night before at Donnie's had been uneventful. Sunny and Gina viewed the wedding picture proofs and helped Leanne decide which ones to select for her album. Reo and Jack showed up after Jack got home from work to share dessert with everyone. Norbert and Donnie traded fishing stories while Buck cleaned the dishes. The evening ended when Norbert nodded off to sleep. When they'd gotten back to Mountain Mist, Norbert asked Buck to come over for breakfast and go for a ride.

They'd turned off the highway twenty minutes ago, just about the time they'd crossed into the next county. The road they traveled was hard-pressed dirt, lined on each side with weather-worn split-rail fence. Broken rails angled sharply to the ground and entire sections of fence were missing. What was this place? Buck had thought he'd explored every road in a twenty-mile radius of Lilac when he was running wild as a teenager. Apparently, he'd missed this particular dirt track.

The car jolted over a rut, thrusting his chest against the seat belt. "Sorry."

Norbert waved it off as if he hadn't even noticed.

Buck slowed down even more, wishing he were driving his Jeep instead of Cole. He shook his head, amazed that the name had stuck. His car was Cole now, christened by Sunny who'd loved driving it as much as he loved driving his Jeep.

Embarrassment spread through him as he remembered Sunny's unexpected hug. His jaw clenched. As much as he might like the feel of her arms around him, he did not want her pity.

Norbert raised his hand and pointed. "Stop at the top of the next hill."

Buck pulled to a stop in front of a rusted out trailer. The windows were broken. Somebody had spray-painted graffiti on the sides. The charred remains of abandoned camp fires dotted the site. Broken bottles glinted in the sun.

Norbert inclined his head. "That's where you were born."

A chill ran down Buck's back. "Say that again."

"Norel showed up one evening with those bikers. I told 'em to set up camp at the pickers' trailer." Norbert snorted. "If it'd been harvest time instead of early spring, they'd have been out of luck."

Buck took in the twisted tree limbs and scrub brush. "What is this place?"

"Apple orchard. Used to be," Norbert said, his eyes sad.

Something didn't sound right. "My birth certificate says I was born at the county hospital."

"Ambulance took you there afterwards. Your grandmother delivered you right here in that trailer. Baptized you, too."

So, his suspicion had been correct. Norbert had recognized the pictures of Carly Day in Donnie's photo album. Buck got out of the car and climbed through the gap in the fence. He thought of the beautiful young woman in the picture, holding a two-year-old Buck on her hip in Donnie's kitchen. He remembered Vegas, his mother's natural charm as she joked with the admiring men at her blackjack table. Anger shot through him at the thought of her laying in a filthy trailer giving birth. He clenched his fists and stomped back to the car. "You couldn't let them stay at the house?"

Norbert's nostrils flared. "Didn't want those bikers anywhere on my property with their drugs and weapons. Only let 'em camp here because of her."

Buck threw the car into gear. "Her name is Carly Day." He bit back the angry words churning inside him, struggling to get his warring emotions under control. Buck had seen biker groups on his trips around the country. Had learned how to recognize the law-abiding riders and keep away from the troublemakers. Isolated out here, away from town, Norbert had to protect himself. Why had Spike gotten involved with a gang? How could he endanger his own father by bringing criminals here?

The dirt road ended at a simple farm house. Buck cut the engine and walked around to the passenger door. "Feet or wheels?"

"Better get the chair," Norbert said, his voice resigned.

Buck's heart softened. Norbert was a proud man who'd insisted on walking on his own two feet to meet his grandson. Buck was certain he wanted to walk on his own two feet now, to enter the home he probably thought he'd never see again. "Use the walker in the house," Buck called out as he pulled the wheelchair from the trunk.

Twenty minutes later, Buck stood on the front porch, wiping the sweat from his brow. He had a whole new appreciation for hospital caregivers. After maneuvering Norbert in the wheelchair up the sloping lawn, he tested the wooden porch with his own weight. He then helped Norbert climb one lumbering step at a time to his waiting walker, all the while hoping the weather-beaten wood hand rail would provide the support Norbert needed.

Norbert fished a key from his pocket and handed it to Buck, his left hand firmly clutching the walker. "Harlan drives out every week or so to check on things. Found somebody camping in the barn a few months back. Called the sheriff to chase 'em off."

Buck unlocked the front door and pushed it open, standing aside as Norbert shuffled in.

"Fetch the metal box from the back seat. And the water," Norbert called as he proceeded into the darkened room. "No power for the well."

Buck hesitated. "Sure you'll be all right?"

Norbert waved him off and plodded forward.

Buck hurried down the hill to the car. He tucked the water bottle under his arm, hefted the metal box from the back seat, and strode across the lawn. He found his grandfather seated at the kitchen table. "You should've waited for me to help you into the chair."

"You sound like one of those nurses," Norbert grumbled. "Give me the box."

Buck leaned against the door jamb. "What if you'd fallen?"

Norbert's stubborn blue gaze locked with his. "Rather fall than be afraid of moving."

"Mule-headed."

The corner of Norbert's mouth curled. "You're not?"

"Didn't say I wasn't." Buck pulled out a chair and sat.

Norbert nodded toward the box. "Four. Twenty-one. Forty-eight. Your grandmother's birthday."

Buck twisted the combination lock until it clicked open and pushed the box across the table.

Norbert's shaking hands reached through the stack of papers, searching. "Four hundred seventy-six acres. Barn to the left. Irrigation pond over the rise. Walk the fence line when you get a chance. Can't know the land until you walk it, my daddy always said." He pulled out an envelope and handed it to Buck. "Original copy of the deed, goes back six generations. Harlan's going to register an updated deed with your name on it at the county courthouse."

"My name?"

"Gabriel Silas Day. Or were you thinking of changing it to Quisenbury?" Norbert's gaze softened. "You're it, son. Last of the line."

"What about Spike?" Buck asked. "You never intended to give all this to him?"

Norbert winced at the sound of his son's nickname. "He never wanted it. And once he passed..." His voice trailed off as he handed a wrinkled stack of papers to Buck. "It's all there. Harlan tracked him down a few years back. Died in prison in California."

Buck pushed away from the table and stood, bracing his hands on the edge of the old porcelain sink. Even through the grimy window, the view from the kitchen was spectacular. Row after row of apple trees, overgrown with intertwined limbs, ran parallel down the sloping field. He tried to imagine his father as a young boy here, running through the rows, tossing apples in the air.

"Why didn't she tell me?" Buck wondered aloud.

"Carly Day? My fault, I reckon. Your grandmother followed the ambulance to the hospital. Told Norel and Carly Day they were welcome to live here, long as they got married and gave up the biker life." His voice sounded far away. "Your grandmother was a good woman. She would've taken those kids in, no questions asked. I added the conditions. Guess I was ashamed my only son turned into a no-good criminal."

Buck watched a myriad of emotions parade across his grandfather's wrinkled face. Wistfulness. Anger. Regret. He crossed his arms and waited.

"Next day, when Marian returned to the hospital, they'd up and left. Broke your grandmother's heart."

"You never saw Carly Day again? Even after she returned to Lilac?" Buck asked.

"Once. Heard she was working as a waitress at The Shoebox. I drove into town and sat at the counter. Knew she recognized me, but her gaze cut me quick, warning me to keep my mouth shut."

Buck knew that look. It was the same one his mother had given him at the blackjack table.

"She'd married Donnie Greene, a fine, hard-working man, as you know. Folks could erase their pasts back then, not like today with people snapping pictures every minute." He scowled. "Didn't want to make a scene, so I paid for my food and left."

"What about later? You must've heard the stories about Professor McNair." Norbert couldn't have missed that juicy bit of gossip, even out here in the countryside. Carly Day became the talk of three counties when she ran off with a British historian researching colonial America.

Norbert nodded. "By then, Marian was sick. Cancer. I was driving her to Charlottesville twice a week for treatment, trying to keep up this place. Wouldn't have been able to raise you the way Donnie Greene could in town. Figured if Carly Day wanted you to know the truth, she would've said something."

Norbert coughed. "Musty in here. Open the back door. Let's have some of that water."

Buck sipped his water in silence. He'd

wanted the truth. A cool breeze blew in, rustling the leaves and carrying the faint scent of apple blossoms. When Norbert had said he wanted to go for a ride in the country, Buck had never imagined they'd end up in an apple orchard. This was crazier than when Reo discovered their grandmother had grown up in the old MacPhee place, right across the street from the Lilac library. Not a soul in town had told Reo or Buck, assuming incorrectly the kids had already known.

What other secrets was Carly Day keeping?

~

Sunny felt a tug on her skirt and looked down.

Nadine's five-year-old daughter Eliza stared up into Sunny's face, her blond hair curling in adorable pigtails around her ears, powdered sugar smudging her cheeks. "Mommy says we need more cups."

Sunny glanced across the crowded church hall.

Nadine stood behind the beverage table. She lifted an empty cup and pointed at it.

Sunny nodded. "Tell your Mommy I'll get her some cups. And give her this." She wrapped a napkin around a cream-filled donut—Nadine's favorite—and handed it to Eliza.

Jim Dobson looked over from the next table where he and his wife were setting out trays of donuts. "Go on and get the cups. Anna and I can finish this."

Anna nodded. "Help Nadine. Only a few

more platters to set out."

Sunny smiled her thanks and turned to face the crowd enjoying St. Andrew's monthly donut social. The atmosphere rang with conversation and laughter, the aroma of fresh coffee wafting through the air. The last mass had just ended and another wave of parishioners was making its way into the hall. She looked around for an opening but folks were packed shoulder to shoulder. She'd never get through the crowd. Sticking close to the wall, she moved as quickly as she could to the storage closet, waving to the folks seated at the tables occupied by Mountain Mist residents. She retrieved two packages of cups and turned around just as Buck pushed Norbert's wheelchair to the seniors' table. Dressed in dark slacks and a starched white shirt, Buck stood stiffly at his grandfather's side, his expression guarded. He looked around as if he were trying to find the nearest exit.

"Morning everybody." Sunny held up the cups and smiled. "I have to run these to the beverage table. Can I get anyone a drink?"

"I'll get you a donut," Buck told his grandfather, his words abrupt. He turned on his heel and walked away.

Was Buck avoiding her? After that awkward hug outside Donnie's house, he hadn't said a word to her the rest of the evening. She watched him disappear into the crowd just like he had at Donnie's cookout after the group picture.

Norbert smiled at her. "Decaf coffee would taste wonderful. Lots of milk."

"Sure thing," she said. She wove through the crowd towards the beverage table. Buck had definitely been preoccupied with news of his father's death when they'd had dinner last week with Donnie and Leanne. Today, he was downright distant. She nibbled her bottom lip, remembering that day at Mountain Mist when he'd said his good manners were all an act. Maybe he wasn't exaggerating. She gave Nadine the stack of cups, fixed Norbert's coffee, and took it to him.

As she was making her way back to the refreshment tables, Mrs. Skokel reached for her hand and pulled her close.

"We were just saying how much we miss Betty Sue," Mrs. Skokel announced. "Nobody can set my curls as well as your mother did." She gave Sunny's hand a pat and released it. The women around the table nodded.

Sunny fought down a twinge of professional jealousy. What was wrong with the way she set curls? Mrs. Skokel had never complained before. "Well, Mom's had a lot more experience than I have."

"Betty Sue was too young to retire," Mrs. Skokel continued, her tone authoritative. "I worked in the cafeteria until I was seventy-two. Would've stayed longer if I hadn't broken my hip."

"Betty Sue told me she hates Florida." Mrs. Carter nodded solemnly, her features pinched with pity.

Sunny froze. Her mother was telling people

she hated Florida?

Mrs. Carter fixed Sunny with a concerned look. "She's also worried about you and." Her wide-eyed gaze pointed to the next table where Buck sat talking with Norbert. The women around the table nodded again.

"Think I'll go see if anybody needs help." Finding the hall air suddenly stifling, Sunny spun around and pushed her way through the tables. Blinking rapidly, she made her way through the crowd, digging her hand into the pocket of her skirt for her car keys as she hurried towards the exit. She couldn't leave. She said she'd help with clean-up. She stepped outside into the midday sun and turned onto the stone walk that led past manicured hedges. At the break in hedges, she entered St. Andrew's contemplation garden and stopped.

The labyrinth was empty.

It's for walking prayer and meditation, their former pastor, Father Matt, had explained when he proposed the project a few years back. At first, some of the parishioners hadn't liked the idea. Many had changed their minds after Father Matt showed them photos of the floor of Chartres Cathedral. Setting the stones in the same labyrinth pattern used in the floor of the medieval French cathedral became a labor of love for the volunteers who'd helped make the contemplation garden a reality. Simple sandstone pavers wound through terracotta-colored bricks, their surfaces smoothed from countless prayer-filled steps. On a beautiful day like today, Sunny would've expected to see children trotting along the circular path while parishioners sat chatting among the blooming plants. But not today. Today she had it all to herself. She inhaled the sweet scent of lilacs and stepped onto the path, following the stones that would take her to the center and back again.

~

A guy didn't have to live in the swamps to know when a dozen sets of eyes were staring him down. Buck was accustomed to alligators peering through marsh grass, not a table full of white-haired octogenarians. When he'd glanced up, the Mountain Mist women had all looked away as if he'd caught them in the act of discussing him.

Like he hadn't experienced that before.

Pretending he hadn't noticed their behavior, Buck excused himself and went into the hallway. He looked in both directions. Whatever those folks had said had sent Sunny racing for the exit. He'd seen her face. Panicked, like she couldn't escape fast enough. Where the heck had she gone? He walked to the left and pushed open the double-doors that led into the church. He glanced around the sanctuary, dim except for the sunlight-illuminated stain-glass window above the altar.

He inhaled the scent of beeswax. Could've knocked him over with a feather when Norbert announced he wanted to come to mass that morning. Carly Day had never said a word about religion. Had she known Spike's family was Catholic, or that Spike's mother had baptized him before the ambulance arrived? He'd always wondered how she'd come up with the name Gabriel. Donnie had read the Bethlehem story to him and Reo every Christmas when they were kids. How Mary and Joseph had to sleep in the stable because there was no room at the inn. Had his mother been thinking about that when she'd given birth to Buck in a beaten-up trailer?

As his eyes adjusted to the dim interior, he noticed a young man kneeling in one of the pews near the front. Even in the faint light, he could tell it was Logan Reed, the new owner of Filmore Hardware that he'd met a few days before. He and Norbert had stopped in to get some oil-based prime sealer for the duck decoy Norbert had carved. The men had hung around the quaint old hardware store for almost an hour, shooting the breeze with Logan.

He backed quietly out of the church and reversed direction, heading for the exit at the other end of the hallway. As soon as he'd arrived this morning, he'd spotted Sunny's car in the lot and had pulled in right beside it. He strode outside and glanced around.

Kermit was still there.

Must've just stepped out for some air. He followed a stone path around the bend of the building and came to a sudden stop. Just beyond the hedge he could see Sunny's head and shoulders, her gaze lowered as if in thought. She walked slowly in one direction then turned and walked around a bend in the direction from which she had just come.

He approached the break in the hedge and glanced inside. Stones created a path of concentric circles that curved back and forth along the same arc, winding to the center then back to the outer perimeter. He'd come upon one of these labyrinths a few years ago in a New Orleans park. He'd read the sign explaining its purpose, describing how similar paths had existed in ancient times. Walking the path supposedly helped people clear their minds. That day in New Orleans he'd sat on a bench near the entrance, watching people quietly entering and leaving. He'd felt a tug to walk the stone path, but in the end had ignored it.

A cool breeze swirled the scent of lilacs around him. He was pretty sure the tug he felt now had little to do with the labyrinth and a lot to do with the woman walking it. In all the years he'd known Sunny, he'd never glimpsed this side of her. The Sunny he knew was always in high gear, smiling and talking with everyone. Joyous, laughing, ready for a joke.

This Sunny seemed lost in thought. Tranquil.

He watched as she took the next turn. The path was leading her to the outer circle. She'd be finished any minute and would see him. He knew he should leave, but his feet wouldn't budge.

He couldn't stop watching if he wanted to.

When Sunny reached the end of the

labyrinth, she glanced up as if coming out of a daze. She gave her head a shake. "Buck." Her voice had a breathy, faraway quality he'd never heard before.

He shoved his hands into his pockets. "Don't tell me you're praying for patience again."

She shook her head. "Just needed a break."

He nodded toward the stones. "You do this a lot? Walk the labyrinth, I mean."

Her eyes widened with surprise.

Probably thought he didn't know what a labyrinth was.

She looked down. "Once in a while."

Great. He hadn't meant to make her feel self-conscious. He gripped the back of his neck. "Is this something Catholics do? I mean, I just found out I was baptized Catholic."

Her eyes widened in surprise. "Are you serious?"

He nodded. It felt weird saying it. He glanced over his shoulder in the direction of the church hall. "Didn't mean to be rude back there. Still getting the hang of this caretaker stuff."

"No worries." Her brown eyes searched his face. "Is everything going okay with Norbert?"

He shrugged. "Considering he told me I was born at his orchard and Spike died in prison, yeah, everything's great."

Sunny shoved her hands into the pockets of her skirt. "Have you ever thought that maybe it was a good thing Spike left?"

His jaw dropped. "You're the first person

who's ever told me being abandoned by a parent could be a good thing."

She raised an eyebrow. "Well, you made it very clear the other evening you don't want sympathy."

His neck felt hot. *She's talking about the hug.*

"I need to help clean up." She hurried past him, head down.

"Wait." He reached out, his fingers brushing the soft skin of her arm.

She stopped. When she lifted her face, her expression seemed guarded. Definitely not the Sunny he was accustomed to.

He blew out a breath. "When I told you that deep down I'm a loner, it's not because I want to be."

Her expression transformed from caution to surprise as her lips parted. "None of us do." She turned and headed toward the church hall.

He watched until she disappeared around the bend then glanced over his shoulder where the labyrinth stones waited. Would anybody see him? Did he care? He entered the circular path, his steps slow. Was he supposed to think or just clear his thoughts? As he walked the stone path, images of overgrown apple trees and a rusty trailer competed in his mind with the faces of Gina, Norbert, and Sunny. He forced himself to look down, reducing his perspective to the ground in front of his feet. Sound became the brush of shoes on stone, smell the faint scent of lilacs.

The path ended abruptly in a small circle. He looked up. An exit path, the same yet different, beckoned.

Chapter Six

"You cut hair here?" Gina asked Monday morning, her gaze darting around the tiny Mountain Mist hair salon.

Sunny ignored the apprehension in Gina's expression. Retirement home phobia. She'd seen it before.

"I told you. I volunteer once a week." Sunny set her tote bag on the counter. "My regular assistant, Colonel Collins, is visiting his daughter in Nashville, so I need you." Sunny grinned. "Buck helped me once."

Gina's eyes flew wide. "Buck worked with you here?"

Sunny nodded. "The morning of Donnie and Leanne's wedding." She sighed. It seemed so long ago. Buck had stood here with her, joking with clients, his anxious gaze scanning faces for one that resembled his own. The news he'd told her about Spike yesterday at the labyrinth must've been a terrible shock. And his words. *I don't want to be a loner.* She'd lain awake half the night pondering them. Was he trying to explain why he hadn't returned her hug?

She unpacked her supplies from the tote bag,

pushing the thoughts to the back of her mind. She wasn't a mind reader. If Buck had something to tell her, he would. "The customers will line up on the chairs outside the door. I need you to greet them and escort them in."

"Escort?" Gina asked, her tone surprised.

"That's right." If Sunny had to guess, she'd say Gina probably hadn't spent a lot of time around the elderly or folks with mobility challenges. "If they're in wheelchairs, ask if they'd like to wheel in themselves, or if they'd like you to push the chair for them. If they're on walkers or using canes, simply walk slowly in front of them and they'll follow."

"Do I need to hold their hands?" Gina didn't look too enthusiastic.

Sunny shook her head. "No, but someone may ask to hold your arm."

Gina gazed through the door into the open lounge area. Some of the residents sat at tables reading. Other's crowded around a corner television. "Everybody looks really old."

Sunny laughed. "They are really old. That's why they live at Mountain Mist." And thank goodness they could. Here they had friends, a sense of community, things that many of them lacked when they had lived alone.

"I left my bottle of lemonade in your car. Can I run out and get it?" Gina's cheeks reddened. "I promise not to drive anywhere."

"Sure." Sunny grinned and handed her the keys. Gina had more than proven her trustworthiness over the past few weeks. She'd completed every task Sunny had given her and been willing to learn new skills. Was Gina aware of how much she'd matured? Was Buck?

Sunny emptied the remaining contents of her tote onto the counter. The extra set of combs she'd packed must've fallen out in the car. She hurried to the door. "Gina!" Her knees bumped into a solid pair of legs.

"Nope." Buck stood in the doorway, his hands settling on her arms to steady her. "Try again."

"Buck!" Her heart skipped a beat. "You surprised me." She searched his face. No scowls. No clenched jaw. Her tense shoulders eased.

Buck stepped back into the hall and rolled Norbert's wheelchair into the room. "Are we first?"

"You sure are." She smiled. "How's it going, Norbert?"

Norbert inclined his head towards Buck. "Be a whole lot better if I could teach this fella to tie a fly."

Buck wagged his hands. "I'm struggling with the finer points of fly fishing."

Sunny smiled. Buck did have big hands. She touched Norbert's shoulder. "Shampoo?"

Norbert nodded. Sunny wheeled his chair over to the sink.

"Hey, Buck." Gina appeared in the doorway with her drink. "Hi, Mr. Quisenbury."

Sunny draped a barber's cloth around Norbert's neck. "Gina's helping me today.

She'll wash your hair while I trim up Buck." She snapped open a second barber's cloth. "What'll it be, Mr. Day?"

"You sure?" Buck hesitated. "I thought you were only here for the residents?"

"And their family members," she added.

Buck grinned. "Give you a big tip."

Her cheeks warmed at the memory of the last time he'd said that to her. They'd still been in their bickering stage. While she was grateful their relationship had moved beyond silly childhood behavior, she no longer knew exactly where they stood. When they'd been together at the labyrinth, she'd felt something between them, an unspoken connection. Had Buck felt it, too?

Buck settled into the barber chair. "Just clean up the neck and sides. The last stylist went a little crazy with the clippers."

She tapped the comb against her palm. "Missing the pirate look, are we?"

"Argh," he replied in a gravelly voice.

Gina giggled.

He gave his sister a surprised look then settled into an easy smile. "Not quite. But maybe you could leave it a little longer on top. I'm getting tired of people saluting me."

Sunny clicked on the clippers, her gaze moving between Buck's profile and his grandfather's. With their eyes closed and faces relaxed, the resemblance was more visible. Similar brow, same strong chin. She'd noticed yesterday Buck hadn't returned immediately to the hall after she'd left him in the garden. Had he walked the labyrinth?

She completed Buck's trim just as Gina was gently toweling Norbert's hair dry.

"Thank you, kindly," Norbert said. "Say, you might be able to tie flies."

"What!" Gina jumped back. Her panicked gaze darted between Sunny and Buck.

Buck burst out laughing. "For fly fishing."

"Ew! You tie flies?" Gina scrunched up her nose.

Sunny brushed Buck's neck clean. "You wrap a hook with different threads and feathers to make it look like a fly. To tempt the fish." She spun Buck around to face the mirror. "My dad and I used to go fly fishing."

Buck's jaw dropped open. "You know how to tie flies?"

Sunny met his gaze in the mirror. She cocked her head. "Maybe."

Buck winked at Norbert then gave Sunny his most charming smile. "What time do you get off work?"

She nibbled her bottom lip. She'd planned on balancing the books this afternoon. Still, Nadine was minding the shop, and Sunny didn't have any clients scheduled. Nadine wouldn't mind closing up. Sunny grinned. "I'm done as soon as I finish here."

Gina peeked out the door. "There's a long line of people."

Buck yanked off the cloth around his neck. "Come on, Gina. Time for the next customer."

Sunny smiled as she listened to Buck introducing Gina to the folks lined up for haircuts. She couldn't believe Buck knew the names of so many residents. He must be spending all his free time at Mountain Mist.

High-pitched giggles sounded in the hall. "Don't let that stern face of his fool you." Norbert said. "That grandson of mine could charm the honey from a bee. No wonder that tour boat business of his is so successful. You know, Anna Skokel gave her secret brownie recipe to the kitchen chef and insisted he make them for Buck."

Sunny laughed. Mrs. Skokel's brownies had been a cafeteria legend. "I hope he shared them with you."

"Better than that. Buck bought enough ingredients so the chef could make brownies for all the residents. Then Buck got the chef to agree to cook one resident's personal recipe every week. They're calling it Friday Favorites."

Amazing. She didn't know what surprised her more: Buck's involvement in the Mountain Mist community or Norbert Quisenbury's talkativeness. He'd spoken more at this appointment than in the two years she'd been cutting his hair and seemed happier than she'd ever seen him.

She gave Norbert's hair one last snip, combed it into place, and removed the cloth. "I'll go get Buck."

Norbert touched her arm, his expression

suddenly solemn. "The Lord blessed me with a grandson later than I would've liked." His voice rasped with emotion. "You be good to him."

"We're not—" she gulped, her protest dying in her throat. Norbert had only seen her and Buck together a few times. Were her feelings for Buck that obvious?

"Nobody knows the day or the hour." His hands moved to grip the arms of his chair, his expression determined. "I won't be around much longer. Don't want Buck to be alone."

Her heart squeezed. She leaned close, pressing a kiss to his wrinkled cheek as she hugged his shoulders. "He won't be," she whispered.

"The list." Buck entered the salon, imitating the way Colonel Collins had presented the list of clients. His tone turned serious. "What's wrong?"

She straightened, wiping her cheeks with the back of her hand. "Nothing."

Buck's gaze moved back and forth between them. He didn't look convinced. "That so?"

Norbert inclined his head but remained silent.

She turned away to wash her hands. "I think your grandfather might be ready for lunch. Who's next?"

"Ms. Wu," Gina announced from the doorway as Sunny's next client steered her walker into the room.

"Are you all right?" Buck stood close at Sunny's side, his voice low in her ear.

She fought an overwhelming urge to rest her head on his shoulder and cry. Was Norbert sicker than he appeared? Had he told Buck? She cleared her throat. "I'm fine. I'll be even better if I can work with my clients." She forced a smile and nodded towards the clock. "Fishing, remember?"

Buck's gaze narrowed. "Something's going on."

Sunny made a big show of glancing around Buck's shoulders and winking at Norbert. "We don't know what you're talking about."

Norbert chuckled.

~

Buck set his phone on the kitchen counter and tapped the speaker button, careful not to smear the screen with his paint-spattered hands. The echo of laughter and kids' voices mingled with the whir of turbines. "Sounds like the scout troop arrived early."

"Give me a minute," Remy shouted over the sudden roar of the boat engine.

Buck heard the muffled stomps of boots on wood followed by a door slamming. "We bumped up the time. Rain's coming later," Remy explained. "How're things going?"

Buck rinsed his hands and dried them. "Busy. This family stuff's taking longer than I thought."

"Nothing bad, I hope." Remy's voice held a note of concern.

Buck glanced around Donnie's kitchen, his gaze lingering on the sink where Sunny had washed his hair. He smiled. "All good. You and Jean-Claude managing okay?"

"Sure. Matter of fact, we have a proposal for you." Remy paused. "We're wondering if you'd like to have some business partners."

"Partners for the *Easy Does It*?" Buck couldn't keep the shock out of his voice.

"Just a percentage. You'd still have controlling interest."

Buck stared out the kitchen window, his gaze fixed on a single robin dipping its bill into the birdbath. His thoughts raced. His gut said no way. He'd built that business from scratch with his own two hands. During the early years, when he'd been putting every penny he had into repairing the *Easy Does It*, the boat had been his home.

Still, Remy and Jean-Claude were hardworking and ambitious. Buck was only able to run the business from a distance because they were there taking care of things. If he refused their request, he might lose his two most valuable crew members.

"Send me your proposal. I'll look it over." Buck hung up, watching as the robin flew off into the distance. The thought of selling even a percentage of the business left a sour taste in his mouth.

Gina strolled into the kitchen. "I'll be giving Sunny my last payment soon."

"That's great," he said. "Congratulations. You set a goal and stuck with it. I'm proud of you."

She leaned against the refrigerator and crossed her arms. "Can we go home now?"

Buck shoved his phone in his pocket. Had she been listening to his conversation with Remy? "I thought you were happy here."

She shrugged. "Working with Sunny is fine. I just thought we'd go back to New Orleans when I finish paying her."

Leave Lilac now? When he was just getting to know Norbert? And Sunny was—Sunny was what?

He saw her in his mind, walking the labyrinth, her features aglow with a tranquil beauty that took his breath away.

Sunny was incredible. He'd been a fool to think his feelings for her had faded. They were stronger than ever.

He cleared his throat. "Your eighteenth birthday is coming up. Don't you want to go out and celebrate with your friends?"

Gina shook her head. "When are we going back?"

He shrugged. "Haven't decided yet."

Her chin flew upward. "Well, could you let me know when you do? I have a life, too!" She stormed outside onto the back porch.

Buck watched through the window as Gina raced around the side of the house. Remy wanted to buy half the business. Gina wanted to go back. Was this all a coincidence, or were the two of them working together?

He fought back the wave of suspicion. No. Remy was an upstanding guy. He would never go behind Buck's back. Gina was just restless—and way too young to get into a serious relationship. She needed to think about getting a job or continuing her schooling.

"Doesn't seem right, you paying me rent and helping me paint." Donnie appeared in the kitchen doorway, his paint-speckled face etched with concern.

Had Donnie heard Gina's outburst? His stepfather had been incredibly patient the past few weeks, never once complaining about Gina and Buck overstaying their welcome when he was trying to get the house ready to sell. Paying rent and helping with chores seemed to be the least he could do. "You're doing Gina and me a big favor by letting us stay on. Wish I could do more." Buck blew out a breath. "Life sure gets complicated when you're taking care of more than yourself."

"No kidding." Donnie chuckled. "Thought I'd have this place ready to sell by the end of June. Every time I finish one project I find five more things that need fixing. Here it is end of July. I'll be back driving the school bus week after next. I'm nowhere near finished, what with the list of things I need to do at Leanne's, I mean *our*, house."

Buck smiled at the slip. Donnie might be a couple decades older, but at the moment he was a newlywed, learning the rhythms of another person's life. "Marriage good?"

Donnie's face lit up with a contented smile. "Best decision I ever made."

"You gonna become Catholic like Leanne?" Buck asked.

Donnie shook his head. "We're going to take turns going to each other's churches. We had some long talks about it before getting engaged."

Buck nodded. Opening up about his personal beliefs to another person scared the heck out of him. Even as a kid, when he'd lived with Donnie and Reo, he'd kept a lot of his thoughts and feelings to himself despite their best efforts to make him one of the family. Had to give them credit. They'd tried.

"I never thanked you," Buck blurted.

Donnie's brow furrowed. "About renting the house? You just did."

"No." Buck's face felt hot. "About everything. Taking me in when you married Carly Day. Raising me after she ran off."

Donnie stared at Buck with total confusion. Then his eyes widened. "Are you watching Dr. Edmund, too?"

Buck set down the towel. "Uh, no. Who's Dr. Edmund?"

"Talk show host. Leanne and I watch his show when she gets home from work." Donnie lowered his voice. "She says watching Dr. Edmund makes her realize the problems she deals with at the DMV aren't so bad."

He could definitely sympathize. Not having to deal with messy emotional problems was one of the things Buck liked best about managing a tour boat. Aside from an occasional bout of sea sickness or a cell phone dropped overboard, conflicts were pretty mundane. Even when he did detect tension between passengers—couples arguing over money, kids defying their parents—the last thing they wanted was for tour boat personnel to get involved.

"Anyway, Dr. Edmund would say you thanking me for raising you and me saying it was my pleasure is a moment of closure. You follow me?"

"Uh-huh." Buck shook off the image of Donnie and Leanne curled up on the sofa eating a platter of raw vegetables, watching a TV therapist.

"Well then, son, it was my pleasure." Donnie slapped Buck on the back and extended his hand. "Let's consider it closed. Deal?"

So, this was what closure felt like. Buck clasped Donnie's hand and smiled. "Deal."

~

The doorbell chimed. Sunny ran up the basement steps, brushing dust from her jeans as she pulled open the front door. "Come in."

Buck followed her inside. "Any luck?"

She shook her head. "Nothing in the garage. I was just starting to look in the basement when you rang the bell." She led the way to the stairs. They needed to find those supplies if they were going to take Norbert fishing.

She'd said a prayer for Buck's grandfather earlier on the drive back from Mountain Mist. Was he sick and keeping his illness a secret? She hoped, for Buck's sake, that Norbert would be around a long time. It would be awful if Norbert were to be taken from Buck so soon after they'd reconnected.

She tried to remember the last time she'd come down here as she descended the steps. Her parents had said they would return sometime to clean out the basement after they got settled in Florida. When she reached the bottom, she rolled her eyes at the floor-to-ceiling clutter. There was enough old furniture and no-longer-used-but-not-ready-to-throw-out items here to fill two houses.

Buck stood at the bottom of the steps, surveying the shelves of boxes in rows across the concrete floor. "Awesome."

She brushed cobwebs off her shoulder. "Awesome? It's embarrassing."

Buck picked up an old percolator and grinned from ear to ear. "Cool. They don't make 'em like this anymore."

"There's a reason for that. Can you remember the last time you drank percolated coffee?" She swatted away a cloud of dust motes as she pulled a box off the shelf. She opened a flap. "Grammy DeStefano's china."

"Let me see." He lifted a scalloped-edged plate and held it up to the light. "It says Havilland. Limoges. Must be a hundred years old."

She wrinkled her nose at the ornate rose pattern and gold trim, gaudy by today's standards. "Nobody eats off dishes like that anymore."

Buck gently set it back into the box. "Perhaps they should."

"You watch those reality antique shows, don't you?" she asked.

"Maybe."

She closed the box lid. "I had to wash each of those dishes by hand every Easter, Christmas, and Thanksgiving. I'll take dishwasher-safe any day." She blew a lock of hair out of her face. "Where is that fishing stuff? I know Dad didn't take it." She rummaged around in the next shelf.

"What's this?" He held up a brass circle.

She glanced over her shoulder. "It's for making an advent wreath."

"What's that?" he asked, examining the four candle holders attached to the ring.

"You put purple and pink candles in the holders. Then you light the candles to mark the four weeks leading up to Christmas."

His brow furrowed. "We never did that growing up."

"It might be more of a Catholic thing."

"Like confession and rosaries? Some of my crew members are Catholic." Buck lifted a basket of stuffed animals. "Yours?"

"Mr. Squiggles!" She pulled the purple-furred rabbit from the basket and squeezed him tight. "He slept on my pillow and sat next to my plate every meal. I dragged him all over the shop while Mom cut hair." She pressed the toy to her cheek and sniffed. "Ew. Moldy." She tossed him back into the basket. "Time for the trash."

She felt Buck's gaze and looked up. He had the strangest expression on his face, like he was offended. She looked around. Dust covered every surface, the air smelled like mildew. Maybe she shouldn't have brought him down here. "My parents are such hoarders."

"You take all this for granted, don't you?" His voice contained a tone she hadn't heard since that night in the sheriff's office. Disappointment.

"Why shouldn't I—oh." Discomfort made her look down. Stuffed animals. Holiday dishes. Outdated gadgets. What looked like forgotten clutter to her represented family history to Buck.

He finally broke the silence. "Don't pity me."

Her head shot up. "Pity?" she sputtered. "I envy you."

"Right." He looked away and lifted the lid on another box.

She could tell by his rigid posture he didn't believe her. "You have brothers and sisters."

"Half brothers and half sisters," he replied dryly. "Don't gloss over the different fathers."

She put her hands on her hips. "And my parents were over forty when I was born. Try imagining what that was like! Always having the oldest parents at school events. Strangers asking if my dad was my grandfather." She threw her arms wide. "Coming to your house, being with you and Reo, was an escape."

"From what?"

He really didn't get it. "If I was at your

house, I wasn't at the shop, entertaining customers or polishing mirrors. Why do you think Reo called me Cinderella?" Memories of her twelve-year-old self staring out the shop window as her friends road past on bicycles came back with a jolt.

Buck stared at her then shook his head. "I guess maybe that old saying is true."

"Which one? About walking a mile in someone else's shoes?"

"No. The one that says forgiveness means giving up all hope of a happy past."

Her lips quivered into a smile. "You mean like accepting my parents are total clutter bunnies?"

The corner of Buck's mouth curved. "Something like that."

She shoved her hands into her jeans, feeling like she was fifteen again and he was seventeen. "I guess that means I have to forgive Mom for telling me I was too young to go to prom with you."

"You actually believed her?" Buck asked.

She stiffened. "Why wouldn't I?"

Resignation shone in the depths of his gaze. "She didn't want you hanging out with me." Buck tucked a strand of hair behind her ear. "Tell me she'd be happy I'm here with you now."

She nibbled her bottom lip. "Dad would be happy we're going fishing," she offered lamely.

"At least you're honest." Buck's lips curved upwards into a lopsided smile. "Be sure to tell your mother I'll be leaving soon."

Her breath hitched. How soon? She lifted her chin. "It doesn't matter what my mother thinks."

"How about the white-haired ladies from Mountain Mist? Don't know what they said, but you bolted from that church hall like a rabbit on the run." Buck slowly traced her cheek, as if he were trying to commit her face to memory. "In a town like Lilac, it matters what people think."

A shiver skittered over her skin.

Her phone buzzed, piercing the silence.

Buck shoved his hands in his pockets and cocked his brow, daring her to check it.

She scowled. She refused to pull out her phone and confirm it was her mother texting again. She wanted to tell Buck she was her own person, capable of making her own decisions, but the words died in her throat.

Because the simple truth was her mother continued to interfere and she let her.

~

Buck climbed off his bike onto the scenic overlook platform, his breathing hard. Main Street lay far below.

"Somebody's out of shape," Jack joked. He relaxed on the bench as if he'd been waiting there all afternoon. The dude hadn't even broken a sweat.

"I'd have won except for that crazy boxer," Buck replied, leaning his bike on the railing next to his brother-in-law's. He'd nearly collided with the gangly brown dog who'd been intent on catching his bike. "Had to stop and help the owner get a leash on him."

"Excuses, excuses." Jack stretched his arms along the back of the bench and closed his eyes.

"You're gonna need to be in shape when the kid arrives," Buck joked. He'd seen firsthand the impact a new baby could have on his crew members. Like working double shifts.

"Can't wait." Jack grinned.

Buck swiped his arm across his brow. When they'd set out for their ride, the sun had been bright above the mountains. Now it barely broke through the clouds drifting across the distant peaks. Nothing like a steep incline to clear the mind. Problem was, as soon as he stopped, he saw Sunny's face again, her chin tilted upwards, her eyes drawing him into their depths. He'd wanted to kiss her and might have if her phone hadn't buzzed.

Jack gave him a serious look. "Reo says I'm supposed to find out what's bothering you."

"She couldn't ask me herself?"

"My words exactly." Jack sipped his water. "She says you keep everything bottled up."

True. He'd protected his little sister as much as an older brother could after their mom had run off. Admitting he might be upset or worried had never been part of the package. "Something wrong with that?"

"Before I started mediator training, I would have said no. But now?" Jack shrugged.

"Don't go using Peacetalkers psychology on me," Buck replied. Jack had started taking advanced negotiation classes as part of his training with the non-profit Peacetalkers, a group that facilitated peace between rival gangs. The long commute to Washington obviously hadn't impacted Jack's workout schedule. He looked as fit as he'd been when he'd played high school football.

Buck dropped onto the bench. "I'm concerned about Gina. I've been hoping she'd find something meaningful to do in Lilac. So far, that hasn't happened."

Jack sipped his water. "Reo and I talked. She's welcome to stay with us again."

"Have you told Gina that?" Buck asked.

"Reo did."

Buck gave the cap on his water bottle a twist. "Let me guess. Gina said no."

Jack nodded.

Great. Like it or not, Buck needed to consider the possibility that Gina might be going back with him. "She's great in the kitchen. Maybe, if I take her back to New Orleans, she'll finally agree to go to culinary school."

"You're not sticking around?"

Why did Jack sound so shocked? Buck shrugged. "Why would I?"

"Your grandfather, for one," Jack observed. "And Sunny."

Buck rose to his feet. His feelings for Sunny were too new, too fragile, to talk about, even with his brother-in-law. "I'll come back to visit. Race you down."

"Reo wasn't kidding. You really do keep things bottled up," Jack said as they headed to the trail.

"My business is a thousand miles away. Managing from a distance only works for a little while. There are things I need to go back and take care of." Buck stored the water bottle in his bike satchel. "Not like I could set up a tour boat business on Cool Water Run."

"True." Jack climbed onto his bike.

They rode down the winding trail and parted ways at the municipal park. As he approached St. Andrew's, Buck steered to the right and followed the road around back. He reached the entrance to the labyrinth garden and stopped.

The pastor, Father Dominic, knelt beside one of the flowerbeds, pulling weeds from the soil and tossing them into a bucket.

Buck hesitated, wishing he hadn't followed his impulse to visit the labyrinth. He'd never encountered a priest dressed in old jeans and a tee shirt before, let alone working on his knees in a garden. A simple dark wooden cross hung around his neck.

Father Dominic saw Buck and sat back on his heels. "Hello," he said, his smile warm. He rose to his feet, pulled off his garden gloves, and extended his hand. His face brightened with recognition. "You're Norbert's grandson."

Buck nodded and shook his hand. Father Dominic's French accent was kind of like the Cajun accents of some of his crew members. Norbert had said he was from Haiti.

"I saw you ride by earlier with Jack Warfield." Father Dominic set his gloves in the bucket. "I had to give up cycling when I injured my back."

"Tough break." Did people gossip with a priest the same way they gossiped with The Shoebox waitresses?

"I settle for brisk walking now," Father Dominic said with a smile, his tone philosophical.

Buck glanced over his shoulder. "Great trail up to the overlook." He'd been impressed by the winding paved path, perfect for hikers and cyclists.

"Did you see the eagles?" Father Dominic asked.

"There are eagles?"

"According to some of the birders in the parish. I haven't caught a glimpse of them yet myself." Father Dominic scanned the evening sky as if he hoped the eagles might just happen to be flying overhead.

Buck stared down at the paved stones, summoning his courage. If he didn't ask now, he may never have another chance. "Has Norbert told you anything about me?" Not exactly the question he wanted to ask, but it was a start.

"A little bit," Father Dominic replied, his expression pleasantly neutral.

"About my father?"

Dominic nodded.

Buck gripped the bike handles tight. "Did

Norbert say anything about my grandmother baptizing me?"

Father Dominic's eyes widened slightly. "Why, no, he did not."

"I was born at the orchard. My grandmother delivered me." Buck stared at the ground, reciting the story as if it was about someone else's life and not his. "Apparently..." He paused and cleared his throat. "Apparently, the cord had been around my neck. She was worried I might die before the ambulance arrived, so she baptized me."

Buck glanced up to see the priest's face break into a wide smile.

"*Mon Dieu!*" Father Dominic exclaimed. "God gave your grandmother the ability to recognize a crisis and to do what needed to be done. You are twice blessed!"

"You mean it counts?" Buck asked, unable to keep the incredulous tone out of his voice.

"Of course, it counts. In times of emergency, any Catholic can baptize a baby in the name of the Father, the Son, and the Holy Spirit. Unless you have renounced the church, you are as baptized as me or your grandfather or anyone."

Buck could feel his lips pull into a wide smile. He was baptized. For years he had wondered, but there had been no one to ask. He didn't know why it mattered so much, but it did.

Father Dominic clasped Buck's shoulder. "God has been with you from the beginning, my son. Never doubt that."

Intense gratitude, deep and unexpected,

closed his throat. Buck nodded. "I won't," he croaked.

Father Dominic glanced at the darkening sky and smiled. "The storm is coming just in time to save my back." He leaned down and picked up his bucket. "I leave the garden to you."

"Does this mean I'm Catholic?" Buck blurted.

Father Dominic nodded solemnly. "Baptism is the first, the most important step."

"There's more to it, isn't there?" Buck asked.

"Yes, there is more." Father Dominic smiled. "Come see me. We will talk."

Relief, deep and profound, settled on him. "I will. Thank you."

"Do not thank me," Father Dominic said as he turned to go. "Thank your grandmother."

~

"Straight back then forward. That's it." Norbert called from his chair beneath the tall oak tree that stood at the edge of Mountain Mist's manicured green lawn.

Sunny watched as the fly she'd tied for Buck bounced against the garden gnome he'd set out as a target. Buck stood a few yards away, moving his fishing rod in time with Norbert's instructions, casting his line again and again.

She grinned. She'd forgotten how much she enjoyed tying flies. Thank goodness, Nadine had agreed to cover for her this morning and open up the salon. She wouldn't have missed this for the world.

Sitting at a picnic table next to Norbert, she surveyed the fly-tying supplies she'd found in the basement: tiny bags of feathers and fur, spools of wire and thread, wire cutters, pliers, and short-nosed scissors. A small vise gripped the edge of the table, holding a fishing hook she had wrapped with gray silk thread. Tiny feather shanks poked out from beneath the thread, giving the appearance of fly wings.

"Which one is that?" Norbert watched her fingers working.

She snipped the last bit of thread. "My dad calls it an Adams Dry Fly."

Norbert held out his hand. "Let me see that." He took off his glasses, held the fly close to his eyes, and nodded his approval. He handed it back. "How about a Caribou Caddis?"

She shook her head. "Never heard of that one."

"Need to get you some caribou hair." Norbert's gaze returned to Buck. "How many times have you hit that thirty-foot marker?"

"Not enough," Buck replied without glancing over, his attention focused on the rod in his hand.

"When you hit thirty feet thirty times in a row, move it to forty feet," Norbert called.

Buck nodded.

She loved watching Buck as he pulled the rod back then angled it forward, his arm movements strong and smooth. There was a steadiness in his motion, an ease that showed both total concentration and total relaxation.

"Still insist you two aren't dating?" Dewey approached the table, grinning at her. His father Frank parked his wheelchair next to Norbert and watched Buck.

"We're friends," she answered firmly, intent on hunting through the supplies for a spool of green thread.

"If you say so. Hey, I didn't know you could do that. Dad, come look at this. Sunny's tying flies."

Frank rolled his chair over to the table.

She felt Frank's gaze studying her creation as she pulled the thread snug. "Have you done this before?"

"Years ago." Frank examined the other flies she'd completed. "Very nice. Ever make a Royal Coachman?"

"No, but I'd love to learn. Want to show me?" She positioned the vise and magnifying glass on the table in front of Frank's wheelchair. She placed a hook in the vise for him while he reached for a spool of wire. His gaze intent on his creation, he worked with silent focus, only glancing up to reach for string or bits of feather.

"You remember." Dewey's voice was filled with wonder. He sat down next to his father, studying his handiwork.

Fascinated, she watched Frank's wrinkled hands confidently wrap the hook.

"Do you have any white duck quill?" Frank asked without looking up.

She rooted through the labeled bags. "I'm not sure."

"How about hen neck?" Norbert asked.

The men launched into a discussion of the merits of various flies and materials, arguing the benefits of natural versus man-made. Buck propped the rod against the table and sat beside her, his face drenched with perspiration. "I hit the gnome thirty times straight. Did you see?"

She bit her lip. "Um, sorry. Missed it."

Buck looked like the kid who hit the home run that nobody saw.

Sunny burst out laughing.

Buck's lips eased into a sheepish grin.

Norbert chuckled and patted Buck's arm. "I saw you. Now move it to forty feet."

"Wait! I want a turn." Dewey snatched the rod and jogged to the center of the lawn.

Buck relaxed in the shade and drank some water while Dewey practiced casting. "I'll take hot mountain sunshine over a humid swamp any day."

"You don't miss it?" she asked, afraid to admit how happy his words made her.

"The swamp? Not right now. Though the critters are more interesting. Can't beat alligators and giant swamp rats for wild entertainment." He turned to Norbert. "Can we go to the river after forty feet?"

Norbert shook his head. "Fifty."

Buck jumped to his feet. "Time's up, Dewey. My rod."

Dewey shook his head, intent on his cast. "Hold your horses. I've got seven straight. Just need twenty-three more."

"What are you, ten?" she teased. Warmth tingled through her as Buck's eyes flashed.

He grinned. "At this moment? Yes. Give it up, Dewey."

She looked over to see Jill Vogel waddling across the lawn toward them. Sunny smiled to herself. Won't be long before the baby arrives.

Jill eased onto the bench next to the table. "That's cool, Frank. What is it?"

Frank removed the hook from the vice and held it up. "That is a Light Cahill."

Jill glanced at Sunny. "Some of the residents would like to join your party. Any objections?"

Sunny glanced at Buck.

He shrugged. "Okay with me. Norbert?"

Norbert nodded. "More the merrier."

Within fifteen minutes, dozens of residents sat in groups on the lawn, watching the casting and fly tying. Sunny grinned as Colonel Collins fetched his fly rod from his room and took over Dewey's lessons. By the end of the afternoon, the gnome marker had been moved to fifty feet, and Buck and Dewey were hitting it consistently. The kitchen staff brought out pitchers of lemonade. Somebody started the gas grill and they were having an impromptu cookout with Mr. Zignetti overseeing the cooking.

Buck collapsed into the shade by his grandfather's wheelchair. "Now can we go to the river?"

Norbert patted his grandson's shoulder. "Another day. I need some shut eye."

Sunny smiled as Norbert yawned. She glanced at Buck. Hands behind his head, he stretched out in the grass and closed his eyes. She watched the steady rise and fall of his muscled chest, the masculine slant of broad shoulders tapering to trim hips. She fought a sudden urge to lean down and brush the damp hair from his forehead.

Could she do it? Start a relationship with a man who had no intentions of staying in Lilac? She snatched up her supplies and shoved them into bags, her hands shaking.

Buck's eyes flickered open. He angled to a sitting position and raked his hand through his hair. "Need some help?"

"No, thanks. It's late. I have to get back to the shop. See you guys later." She jumped to her feet and hurried across the lawn.

She'd been an idiot to open her heart to Buck. He was leaving. Returning to his tour boat business. If only they could go back to their silly teasing and pranks. Maybe then the thought of him going away wouldn't hurt so much. She blinked the moisture from her eyes as she rounded the corner of the building.

"Sunny, wait up!" Jill called.

Sunny steadied her breath and slowed her pace as she waited for Jill to join her.

Jill folded her arms on top of her stomach. "How would you like to teach a fly tying class?"

"Me?"

Jill motioned to the groups of seniors sitting around the lawn. "You did great, helping the seniors this afternoon."

"I was just having fun," Sunny said.

"You're a natural instructor. And you'll be paid." Jill held up her hand. "Don't protest. We hire instructors all the time to teach." Jill explained the rates Mountain Mist paid for the various types of classes.

That was more per hour than Sunny made cutting hair at the Up Do. "Sure, I'd love to teach."

"Great. You can start next week."

Sunny shook her head in wonder as she walked to her car. What was that saying of Father Dominic's about the God of surprises? Here she was, caught up in her own sadness about Buck leaving. She never would've expected Jill to invite her to teach a class—yet doing something like teaching would be exactly what she'd need after Buck left. And there was no use denying it. Buck was going to leave.

Resigned to the truth, she stored the bags in the passenger seat and retrieved her phone from the glove box. She scrolled quickly through her messages. Six from her mother before noon. That had to be a new record. She sighed. She used to think answering every one of her mother's messages was a pain, but that was nothing compared to the nightly phone conversation where she had to recap all the business of the day.

She opened a text from Reo.

Come to Leanne and Dad's house tonight at seven.

Sunny grinned, her mood brightening at the invitation. *What's up?*

I'm surprising Dad.

Sunny tapped a quick reply, her thoughts racing. *What kind of surprise?*

Chapter Seven

"**What do you** think the surprise is?" Gina asked as Buck parked in front of Leanne's townhouse.

Buck gave his head a shake. Make that Leanne and Donnie's townhouse. "With Reo, you never know."

"Reo was talking about getting a puppy. You think it's a puppy?" Gina sounded excited. "Hey, there's Sunny."

He glanced up to see Sunny walking towards them. Her billowy pink dress clung to her slender curves, swirled around her tanned legs. She raised her hand to wave.

Buck felt a sudden pang in his gut as he watched her approach. Remy had called earlier to tell him their paper products supplier announced she was going out of business. On top of that, a pleasure boater had rammed the dock with his boat and damaged some of the boards. He couldn't leave all these things for Remy to fix. He'd have to go back and take care of it. The thought of leaving Sunny suddenly made it feel like someone had placed a large rock on his chest.

Gina hopped out of the car and ran to Sunny. "You think Reo got a puppy?"

He climbed out and watched as Sunny put her arm around Gina's shoulders. He couldn't hear what they said to each other, but a minute later Gina exclaimed, "Well, Snow White does love animals," and ran up the steps into the townhouse.

He joined Sunny on the sidewalk. "Any idea what this is about?"

Sunny shook her head, her eyes bright with excitement. "Must be important if Reo's calling us all over."

As they climbed the steps, he rested his hand on the small of Sunny's back, the fabric of her dress smooth beneath his fingers. "Everything all right at the shop?"

Her brow furrowed. "Sure. Why wouldn't it be?"

"You hurried away from Mountain Mist awfully quick this afternoon. Thought there might be a problem." They stood so close he heard her breath hitch.

"No problem." Her smile brightened. "When I was walking to my car, Jill asked me to teach a weekly fly tying class at Mountain Mist."

"That's great. Worried what your mother will say?" he asked.

"I hadn't thought of that yet, but thanks for bringing it up." She gave him a mischievous grin.

He stepped to the side and pulled open the

screen door. "Let me know if there's anything—Leanne, what's wrong?"

Leanne welcomed them wordlessly, tears running down her cheeks.

Buck scanned the room, looking for the source of Leanne's tears. He spotted Donnie sitting next to Reo on the corner loveseat, both of them staring at the phone resting in his sister's palm.

"It's not a puppy," Gina muttered as she dropped into an armchair.

Reo handed Donnie the phone and ran to them. "It's a boy!" She threw her arms around Buck and Sunny, pulling them both into a hug. "I didn't get a chance to break the news to Dad about the baby. I wanted to make sure I told him in person we're having a boy."

"Did Donnie cry?" Sunny whispered.

Reo shook her head. "He's still in shock."

Buck gripped Reo's shoulders and eyed her up and down. "Now, you look pregnant." He gave his sister a hug. "Where's Jack?"

"Taking an exam. He wanted to be here." Reo kissed Buck's cheek. "Can you believe it? We're having a boy."

"Do we get to see the little guy?" Buck asked.

"If I can pry the phone away from Dad." Reo grinned.

Donnie handed the phone to Reo, a look of wonder on his face. "A boy."

Leanne stood in the middle of the room, fanning her face with her hands. "I get so emotional about this kind of stuff." She sat beside Donnie and kissed his cheek. "Congratulations, Grandpa! You've got a new fishing buddy."

"Now, he's crying," Reo whispered.

Gina, Sunny, and Buck crowded around the phone. Buck studied the tiny black-and-white image. He could see the form of a baby clear as day. His nephew.

"Look, he's sucking his thumb," Sunny cooed in a sweet little voice he'd never heard before. "I'm so happy for you. Tell me I get to give him his first haircut."

Reo grinned. "Think I'd trust anyone else?"

Buck couldn't take his eyes off the picture. He'd seen sonogram images before, but never the sonogram of a family member. He glanced at Sunny, drawn to the expression of pure wonder on her face. An unfamiliar yearning stirred somewhere deep inside him.

Sunny glanced up. "You feeling all right? You look kind of pale."

"Just remembered something," he muttered, glancing away. He pulled out his phone. "Excuse me." He strode out the front door and down the walk. Once inside his car, safe behind the tinted windows, he tossed his phone onto the passenger seat, his heart pounding. What was the matter with him? It was a tiny picture of his tiny nephew. A new little life coming into the family. Surely that was causing the sharp pangs of protectiveness and longing surging inside him. He closed his eyes. He shouldn't have glanced up. The instant he saw the look of awe on Sunny's face, a sense of certainty had exploded within him.

He wanted a family of his own. With Sunny.

Kids. A house. A dog and a minivan. He could see it all.

What the heck was the matter with him? He'd never once in his entire life thought about settling down.

~

Buck couldn't shake the thought. Not when he went to bed that night. Not when he was visiting with his grandfather the next day. Images tormented him as he pushed his grandfather's wheelchair along the shaded path. Sunny. A family. Who was he kidding? He didn't know the first thing about being a father. Look how clueless he'd been with Gina.

Plus, he lived a thousand miles away.

He pushed his grandfather's wheelchair into the small air conditioned apartment.

"Been thinking about something." Norbert rose to his feet, gripped his walker, and turned to face his grandson. "I want to move back home."

"To the orchard?" Buck asked, surprised. "I thought you liked it here."

"Being resigned to something ain't the same as liking it," Norbert replied, his expression somber.

Buck's gaze shot around the apartment, his thoughts racing. With a floor plan and furnishings resembling a basic hotel suite, the place felt clean but sterile. He couldn't blame Norbert for wanting to go home, but they had to be reasonable.

Norbert watched him, intent as a hawk. "Thought maybe you could take over the orchard. Make it produce again."

"Is that why you signed the property over to me? You thought I'd move back?" When Norbert didn't answer, Buck frowned. He'd thought his grandfather had only wanted to pass on the family legacy when he mentioned putting Buck's name on the deed. Did Norbert also want Buck to become his full-time caregiver? Had he given Norbert false expectations by accepting his gift?

Norbert sat down. "No. The orchard is yours. Just thought you might consider moving back."

Buck raked his hand through his hair. His grandfather wanted them to live together. Guilt shot through him as he crossed the room and gripped Norbert's shoulder. "You caught me by surprise. Can we talk more about this later?"

Norbert nodded as he lowered into an armchair, his gaze fixed on the endless blue sky outside the window.

Buck strode from the room and hurried down the steps, making a beeline for the main entrance. His heart thumped loudly in his chest. This was his fault. If he hadn't been so excited about connecting with his long lost grandfather, Norbert would be content with his life at Mountain Mist. He wouldn't be sitting upstairs now wanting something that wasn't possible.

He never should've come back and stirred things up. He'd arranged his life so that he didn't have to rely on anyone.

Or have anyone rely on him.

"There you are." Sunny waited on a bench outside the front entrance. She jumped to her feet, her white sun dress swirling, her eyes bright. "I can't believe it! Dr. Dalir just asked if I'd like to take over as Activities Director when Jill goes on maternity leave next week."

He took Sunny's bag of hair styling supplies and led the way across the parking lot. "You're already cutting hair and teaching. Will you have time?"

"Activities Director is a part-time position. I can schedule my salon clients around the hours I need to be at Mountain Mist. A lot of the activity scheduling work I can do remotely. Like you do." Sunny gazed up at him, her smile radiant.

Should he attempt to do more work remotely so he could stay in Lilac longer? His thoughts rushed. He needed to go back. He couldn't dump those dock repairs on Remy. He glanced over his shoulder, guilt gnawing at him. Was Norbert still sitting by the window, staring at the sky? Did he really think his grandson could just give up his tour boat business and move in with him? His forehead broke out in a sweat. He didn't know the first thing about taking care of an elderly person. Look what a mess he'd made of trying to take care of a teenager—and he'd been one of those.

"Hey." Sunny touched his cheek. "What's wrong?"

Her cool fingers soothed his hot skin, eased his anxious thoughts. He didn't deserve the kindness she offered, yet he drank it in like a man dying of thirst.

"Earth to Buck." She got up onto her toes and touched her lips to his.

Her kiss sent a shockwave through him. He angled his lips to hers, every nerve suddenly alive. When she moaned and slid her arms around his waist, his years of pent-up yearning exploded in one passionate realization.

She wanted him. As much as he wanted her.

"Woohoo!" a voice shouted behind them.

"You go girl!"

"Finally!"

He lifted his head and glanced around. A group of seniors stood in line clapping and cheering as they prepared to board a shuttle bus.

Sunny laughed and waved. "We have an audience."

"Tell me about it." Keeping one arm wrapped firmly around Sunny, he raised his other hand in a stiff wave.

Sunny stared at him and tilted her head. "This kind of attention is difficult for you, isn't it?" she asked softly.

"You have no idea," he said out of the side of his mouth.

She wrapped her arms around his waist and rested her cheek against his chest. "Better get used to it."

The awkwardness he felt didn't exactly go away, but having Sunny's arms around him helped to ease the self-consciousness.

"Friends," Dewey scoffed as he approached. "Right."

Sunny bit her bottom lip as Dewey passed. "I told him the other day we were just friends."

Buck stiffened. "Is that what you want?"

~

Sunny shook her head. "No." The transformation of Buck's expression, from wariness to joy, took her breath away. Her heart skipped into high gear as she and Buck hurried across the parking lot, stopping to kiss again. And again. She smiled. "Really? You had no idea how I felt?"

"None." His face practically glowed with relief. "Told you. I'm a socially awkward swamp dweller."

"You are not. You're just very private," she said as they slipped into his car. She'd always known Buck was quiet, but she realized now it was more than that. Whenever he'd teased her in the past, they'd been alone, away from the watchful eyes of Lilac residents. Even when they'd been kids, if Donnie and Reo had been around, Buck would be more reserved, as if he didn't want to show his emotions when others were present.

"Probably more like clueless." He traced her cheek with his finger as he gazed into her eyes. "You know how to read people."

The corner of her mouth curved upward as she slid her hands around his neck. "Read this," she said as she pulled his head down to hers. His lingering kiss took her breath away.

"Thank God for tinted windows," he murmured.

Sunny ran her hand through his hair, loving the silky feel beneath her fingers. "Doesn't like having an audience. Check."

"It's more than that." Buck started the engine and drove out of the lot. "I'm an outsider. You're used to all this."

Sunny tilted her head, confused. "Used to what?"

He motioned at the passing streets. "Letting everyone into your personal life. Being on display."

"That's just part of living in a small town," she protested.

He shook his head. "If you like being constantly judged."

Was that what this was all about? "Nobody's judging you."

He glanced at her, his gaze tinged with regret. "Sorry, but that's where you're wrong."

Sunny stared out the window. How could she get through to Buck that nobody cared about his family's past? The residents of Mountain Mist liked Buck for who he was. They'd welcomed him into their community. Couldn't he see that?

She linked her fingers with his. "I can see I'm going to have my work cut out for me."

"What's that supposed to mean?" he asked.

"We DeStefano's are a touchy-feely bunch. Hugging and kissing all the time. And we don't care who sees. You gonna have a problem with that?"

"Not as long as you're the one I'm hugging and kissing." He grinned.

She closed her eyes. Hope. For the first time, she had hope they could work things out despite the distance from Lilac to New Orleans. *Thank you, God.*

They turned onto Main Street and came to a sudden stop. Why was traffic backed up in the middle of the day?

"Uh-oh." Buck pulled the car to the curb and parked in front of Deutsch's Furniture.

A fire truck's spinning red light bounced off the shop fronts, making Lilac look like one of those unknown towns that suddenly appear on the news because of some unexpected disaster. People stood in clusters on the sidewalk, watching.

"It's the Up Do!" Sunny jumped from the car and ran down the sidewalk.

Buck jogged with her past The Shoebox. "I don't smell smoke," he shouted.

Relief coursed through her as she inhaled the smoke-free air. Thank God. No smoke. People called her name, but she pushed through the crowd, refusing to stop. Water splashed on her bare legs as she ran through the puddles.

"Where were you?" Gina cried, wet hair plastered to her head, her tank top and blue jeans dripping. "A pipe burst."

Water ran from the Up Do entrance onto the sidewalk. Sunny's heart raced. She scanned the scene. "Was anybody hurt?"

Gina shook her head, her expression frantic. "Nadine left early to get her kids. It was just me and Billy in the shop."

Sunny looked at the muscular young man in the drenched tee shirt standing beside Gina. His hair was buzzed short except for one stringy patch behind his right ear.

"Gina's cutting hair now?" Lavinia approached, eyeing the two teens. "Does she have a license?"

"No, she doesn't," Sunny admitted, her jaw tight.

"Betty Sue would never allow that," Lavinia snorted.

"I tried to call you and ask," Gina shot back, her tone defensive.

Sunny winced. "I'm sorry. I didn't hear my phone."

Gina whirled on Buck, anger and frustration fused in her gaze. "You didn't answer your phone, either."

"My battery's dead." Buck angled a questioning look at Sunny. "We were at Mountain Mist."

Sunny clenched her fists. This was all her mother's fault. If Betty Sue hadn't been calling and texting so much, Sunny wouldn't have had to keep her phone on silent. She could have been here to help Gina.

"A pipe burst in the ceiling." Sheriff Dobson joined them, wiping his brow with a handkerchief. "Firemen turned off the main valve. They're checking for electrical damage. Good thing Gina called 9-1-1 as quickly as she did."

Sunny stifled a groan. A call to 9-1-1 meant an automatic call to the security company.

And an automatic call to the property owners.

Lavinia wagged her phone in Sunny's face, diamond rings flashing in the sun. "Betty Sue just texted. She wants to know why you're not answering your phone."

~

"One, two, three, lift." Buck and Jack hefted the styling station up the front porch steps of the MacPhee house. They carried it into the front room and set it down on the bare wood floor. A group of high school boys entered behind them, carrying linens, hairdryers, and styling supplies. "Bottles on the shelves. Towels in the baskets," Buck directed, pointing at the salon storage units standing in the corner.

Jack dropped into a chair. "Last of the heavy furniture," he said.

"Great idea, asking the football team to help." Buck wiped his brow.

"Didn't have to," Jack said. "When I called Coach Jefferson to ask about borrowing his pickup, he insisted on bringing the seniors over. Think he felt bad about Gina getting in trouble for cutting the hair of one of his players."

Buck glanced around. Speaking of Gina, where was she? It had been a couple hours since she'd gone home to change out of her wet clothes.

"Leave those damp cushions on the front porch to dry out." Sunny's voice drifted inside through the open window.

Buck watched as Sunny stood at the front gate, joking with Coach Jefferson and a few of the players. He couldn't believe how calm she was. Just like when Gina had wrecked her car. After getting over the initial shock and reassuring her parents that the water damage wasn't too great, she'd taken charge, making the decision to open up the MacPhee house and move all the salon furnishings over there so that the Up Do could dry out. It was as if she were drawing on some silent inner strength that helped her to remain cool and collected.

"That can go in the back room," Sunny advised a young man carrying a large mirror. "And please be careful."

Jack jumped to his feet and ran onto the front porch. He reappeared with Reo by his side, a basket of magazines in his hands. "You're not supposed to carry anything heavy."

"Six magazines in a basket is not heavy," Reo protested. She looked around the room, hands on her hips. "So, this was our maternal grandmother's childhood home."

Buck nodded. "Yep. Carly Day's mom was raised here. To think we both grew up in Lilac and never knew." He scanned the scuffed wood floors and cracked plaster walls. Dust-caked light fixtures hung from the ceiling.

Reo walked around, studying the surroundings, as if she were trying to imagine how the room once looked. "I wouldn't have found out if Jack hadn't convinced Harlan to move the old newspaper archives from his attic to the library."

"Score one for the mediator." Jack grinned.

"Think Carly Day spent time here?" Buck asked.

Reo shrugged. "Who knows?"

"Still angry she didn't come to your wedding?" Buck asked.

"After what you told me she said to you and Gina in Vegas?" Reo shook her head. "If Carly Day didn't want people to know she was a mother, do you think she's going to want them to know she's a mother-in-law? Or a grandmother?" Her voice sounded hollow, like she no longer cared, or at least had tried to convince herself she didn't. She checked her phone. "Gina should be here. I texted her to say we're helping Sunny. I hope she isn't sitting home moping."

"It was just bad luck. That pipe could have burst at any time." Buck pulled out his phone and tapped open the app for Pizza Mountain. "Tell her we're ordering pizza. That might get her over here. I'm thinking ten extra larges."

"Better make it an even dozen," Jack replied as he reached for Reo's hand. "Somebody's eating for two."

Reo grinned. "Maybe three."

Jack blanched. "What did you say?"

"Gotcha!" Reo gave Jack a smug look followed by a kiss on the cheek.

Buck's gaze moved to the open window. Sunny now stood talking with Lavinia. He cleared his throat. "You know Sunny's parents better than I do. Are they going to freak out about this?"

"Vince will be okay. He's mellowed since the heart attack. Betty Sue's another story. I'm sure she was upset about the burst pipe." The corner of Reo's mouth curved. "But not as upset as she's gonna be when she learns you two are dating."

"Did Sunny tell you we're dating?" he asked.

Reo's gaze softened. "Didn't need to. Anybody can see you two are crazy about each other."

Buck shoved his hands in his pockets. A twinge of embarrassment, like the one he'd felt when the Mountain Mist residents were applauding him and Sunny, settled uneasily on his shoulders. Did everybody already suspect what he was just figuring out?

Jack rose to his feet and slapped Buck on the back. "Don't look so glum. Betty Sue probably already knows."

Buck frowned. "And probably doesn't like it one bit."

Reo linked her arm through Buck's and rested her head on his shoulder. "Forget Betty

Sue. The important thing is you and Sunny are happy."

174

Chapter Eight

Sunny shoved the push broom, sending a spray of water drops through the entrance onto the sidewalk. Despite the open windows and whirring ceiling fans, damp air permeated the salon. Gripping the end of the handle, she rested her chin on her hands, studying the full moon above the mountains. They'd been working all afternoon and through the evening. It must be getting close to eleven p.m. She sighed. "I should have given Gina the day off."

Buck took the broom from her hands and led her to the back office. Miraculously, the small room and its contents were completely dry. He sat beside her. "We've been over this. Gina is my responsibility. I wasn't available when she needed me."

The flooding of the shop didn't bother Sunny half as much as the look of betrayal on Gina's face. Broken pipes could be replaced. But broken trust? "If only I'd told Gina and Nadine where I was going."

He leaned forward, elbows on his knees, staring at the floor. "Why didn't you?"

She sucked in her cheeks. "I haven't told my

mom yet about the teaching job at Mountain Mist. I didn't want Gina or Nadine spilling the beans."

He straightened, a look of relief on his face. "I thought maybe you didn't want anyone to know we were spending time together."

"Wrong again." She linked her arm through Buck's and rested her head on his shoulder. He'd been at her side every minute. Cleaning up the mess, directing the volunteers, ordering food for everyone. "I couldn't have managed without you. I wish my mom was here. I'd tell her how wonderful you've been through all this." She tilted her face up to his, her breath catching as he leaned closer.

His gaze suddenly fixed on something beyond her shoulder. He cleared his throat. "Got your wish."

She glanced around. Her parents stood framed in the entrance. Vince, wearing the khakis and blazer her mother insisted he wear when they traveled, smiled at her. Betty Sue, looking stylish but exhausted in her dove gray pant suit, stared at them open-mouthed.

What were they doing here? "Mom!" Sunny leaped to her feet and raced across the salon. Her shoe hit a patch of slick tile. Arms flailing, she tumbled backwards.

"Watch out." Buck's strong arms locked around her waist before she hit the floor, pulling her tight against his chest.

Betty Sue gasped.

"You changed your hair," Sunny sputtered,

settling her feet on the floor and squirming out of Buck's arms. Her mother's hair had gone from ash brown to bleached blond since their move to Florida.

"Think I lost some," her father chuckled, running a hand over his bald head. "Speaking of lost, what happened to all the furniture?"

Sunny made her way cautiously across the damp floor as if she were walking on ice. "It's over at the MacPhee place drying out." She kissed each of her parents. "What are you doing here?"

"Your mother said you needed us. Pretty obvious you have help." Her father took a careful step forward, arm outstretched. "Vince DeStefano."

"Buck Day." Buck shook Vince's hand.

Vince's face broke into a warm smile of recognition. "Well, I'll be. Look, Betty Sue, Reo's brother Buck."

Betty Sue stared at them as if they were aliens.

At least her mother had closed her mouth. Sunny reached for Buck's arm and tugged him forward. "Buck, you remember my mother."

"Sure do. How are you doing, Mrs. DeStefano?" he asked, his tone polite.

Betty Sue regained her composure enough to nod a brief acknowledgment. "We're fine."

Sunny gave Buck a weak smile, hoping he didn't realize her mother was using the same voice she used with telemarketers.

Betty Sue glanced around. Her face

suddenly pinched up as if she smelled rotten cheese. "Where did those curtains come from?"

"I bought them." Sunny lifted her chin, readying herself for her mother's criticism of the brightly-colored fabric hanging across the window. "They look much better when they're dry."

Betty Sue pressed her lips tight as if she were fighting the urge to say what she really thought.

"Must've been a lot of working, moving all the equipment next door," Vince spoke up, breaking the awkward silence.

Buck shrugged. "Not too bad. The high school football team volunteered to help."

"You allowed minors to help?" Betty Sue's eyes flew wide. "What if someone had gotten hurt? The salon would have been liable."

"Nobody got hurt." Sunny frowned at Betty Sue's shrill tone. Why did her mother always focus on the negative?

Betty Sue gave Sunny a pointed look. "It's been a long day. I think it's time we went home."

And Sunny was just supposed to jump because her mother commanded it? Enough was enough. Sunny stepped to Buck's side. "Fine. We'll see you tomorrow." Let her mother deal with that.

Buck stood stock still. "I don't think—"

Sunny searched Buck's face. "I know what you're going to say. Opinions matter in small towns. People gossip. I have to take a stand."

She locked gazes with her mother.

Betty Sue looked away.

Adrenaline shot through Sunny. She felt like she'd hiked to the top of a mountain. She'd never felt so exhilarated. She was finally going to be free of her mother's interference. She would stand up for herself, do what she believed was right no matter what her parents thought.

Sunny headed for the door, Buck's hand tight in hers. She came to a sudden stop. "Gina!"

Buck's little sister stood in the doorway. She wore the short denim skirt and tie-died tank top she'd worn the first day she'd arrived in town. Her eyes didn't look puffy from crying any more. In fact, she looked happy.

"I came to say goodbye." She motioned over her shoulder. "My mom's waiting for me."

"Who?" The word exploded from Buck's lips.

Sunny whirled around and stared at Buck's face, his expression even more shocked than when he'd learned about Norbert. She gulped and released his hand.

Betty Sue gaped through the window. She fanned her finger at Vince. "Come here. Look."

Vince remained where he was, his concerned gaze moving between his wife and his daughter.

Sunny peered into the summer night, trying to catch a better glimpse of the beautiful woman waiting in the shiny white convertible, her profile illuminated in the streetlight's glow. Her long blond hair curled in perfectly layered tresses over the collar of her red leather jacket. One red nail tapped the steering wheel.

"What's Carly Day doing here?" Buck stomped to Gina's side.

"She's taking me to New Orleans." Gina's voice bubbled with excitement. "I called her."

"You what?" Buck raked his hand through his hair. "Have you forgotten how she treated us in Vegas? She hasn't called you since."

"She's been busy..." Gina's voice trailed off.

Buck gripped Gina's shoulders. "Listen to me. Please. You can't depend on her."

"I can't depend on you, either," Gina wailed as she stepped away from her brother and crossed her arms. "I wanted to go back to New Orleans and you wouldn't take me. We're getting casino jobs. Mom knows people."

Sunny watched the play of emotions on Buck's face—shock, outrage, anguish. Then he went still as a statue, all emotion fleeing as the mask he showed the world slipped back into place. When he finally gazed at Sunny, his features were like carved stone. "I have to deal with this."

Sunny pressed her lips together and nodded.

Buck faced her parents. "Good night, Mr. and Mrs. DeStefano." He strode outside.

"Here's the last of the money I owe you." Gina pushed a wad of bills into Sunny's hands. "Sorry all this happened." She scurried out the door after Buck.

Sunny's heart constricted as she watched

Buck and Gina climb into Carly Day's car, the women animated, Buck stone-faced. She blinked. She'd failed Gina and lost Buck. Maybe she should've minded her own business instead of getting involved in theirs. She wouldn't be feeling this awful pain in her heart if she had stayed out of it.

"Sunny?" Her father finally spoke, his tone worried.

Sunny shook her head, refused to look at him. She would not walk into the comfort of her father's open arms. She wasn't a little girl anymore who could be consoled with Daddy's hugs and simple words. With or without Buck, she had to stand on her own two feet, make her own choices and be accountable for them.

Betty Sue tapped her cell phone, her eyes sparkling with excitement. "Lavinia! You'll never guess—"

"Betty Sue!" Vince barked.

"We just got back," Betty Sue whispered into the phone. "I'll call you tomorrow."

Vince straightened to his full height, his dark gaze moving between his wife and his daughter. "My blood pressure thanks you for keeping all this drama a secret." He gave them both a steely gaze. "Settle this before you give me a second heart attack."

Betty Sue took a step toward Vince, her expression panic-stricken.

"I'm going to The Shoebox," he announced, his voice stern. He walked outside.

Betty Sue stared at the empty doorway a

moment and then whirled around, her expression livid. "I knew something like this would happen."

Sunny's jaw dropped. "You knew a pipe would burst?"

Betty Sue made a face. "It's bad enough you let Gina drive your car and she wrecked it, but cutting hair without a license! What were you thinking?"

"It only happened once." Sunny struggled to keep her voice calm. "She was trying to help a boy on the football team. Coach told him he had to get his hair buzzed before he could step onto the practice field."

Betty Sue raised her cell phone and shook it. "My phone's been ringing off the hook since we moved to Florida. Do you realize how many people called to tell me Buck Day climbed out of your back seat buckling his belt? And what were you thinking, driving around town in his expensive sports car?"

Sunny gritted her teeth. Why did her mother spend so much time worrying about what other people thought? "I can't control gossip."

"But you can make better choices." Her mother threw up her hands. "You never turned in the list of promotional items to Lavinia. You permitted Nadine to arrive late and leave early. You allowed high school students to work on water-damaged premises. I told your father I didn't think you were ready to manage."

Sunny felt the words like a slap. She curled her fingers into her palms. She'd spent her entire life preparing for a single moment: taking over the family business. Her parents had begun grooming her as soon as she could walk and talk. Entertaining customers when she was three. Sweeping the floors when she was eight. Shampooing hair when she was twelve. And always, always, above everything else, worrying about what other people thought.

"You're right. I quit." Sunny ran from the shop, sandals slapping on the sidewalk. Blood pounded in her ears as she raced across the empty street and down the block. She'd done it. She'd quit. Her mother was not going to control her life anymore. Oh, Betty Sue would deny that she had any influence over her daughter, but she did, in so many ways. In too many ways.

Sunny wiped her eyes. Buck had been right when he'd said her mother didn't know how to delegate. And critical! Why did she have to be so critical? Was that why Buck had hesitated when she'd stood up to her mother? He didn't want to deal with Betty Sue's sharp tongue? Maybe he'd been relieved when Gina and Carly Day had shown up and offered him a way out of the awkward situation.

She needed to talk with Reo. Her best friend would understand. She stopped. She couldn't go to Reo's house. For all she knew, Buck, Gina, and Carly Day were there right now, having a family reunion.

She slowed her pace, swatting at the angry tears that burned her eyelids. The days of her mother's meddling were over. No more living in

Betty DeStefano's shadow. No more putting up with her criticism, her judgmental comments about Sunny's friends. She was perfectly capable of living her life without her mother's constant interference. Throwing her shoulders back, she spun on her heel and marched in the opposite direction, past the Up Do and Sparkles Galore. She yanked open the door to The Shoebox and strode inside.

The diner was packed and buzzing with the Friday night crowd. Lulu greeted her with a sympathetic smile. "Hey, Sunny. Sorry to hear about the burst pipe. Your parents are over by the window." She motioned for Sunny to follow her.

"No, thanks. I'll sit here." Sunny plopped onto a red vinyl stool at the counter and flipped open a menu.

Lulu froze mid-step. She looked at Sunny's parents then back at Sunny. "Uh, sure." She whipped around and hustled behind the counter. "You okay?" she whispered, leaning close as if she didn't want the other customers at the counter to hear.

"I'm great," Sunny announced in a loud voice, flashing a big smile. "In fact, I'm celebrating Independence Day a few days late. I just quit my job."

"Job? You mean the Up Do?" Lulu's eyebrows almost touched her hairline. "You quit the Up Do?"

Sunny nodded. "I think that calls for pie. What do you have?"

"Peach and blueberry. But you're the Up Do manager."

"Not anymore. I'll take blueberry."

Lulu retrieved the pie and set a piece in front of Sunny. "Who's going to manage the Up Do?"

"I don't know, and I don't care." Sunny jabbed the pie, her fork clattering against the plate. Why had it taken her so long to figure out she didn't have to be at her parents' beck and call?

"You're parents are staring. They don't look happy," Lulu whispered.

"I'm sorry to hear that." Sunny forked a mouthful of pie between her lips and swallowed. Let them stare. Maybe they'd finally realize she wasn't a little girl anymore. "This is delicious. May I have some water, please?"

"Sure." Lulu filled a glass and set it on the counter. "Betty Sue looks like she's going to be sick."

Sunny sipped her water. Served her mother right for being such a control freak. Dress neatly. Be polite. Remember we're in business. Well, Sunny wasn't in business anymore. The sooner her parents realized that the better.

Lulu craned her neck. "Vince's ears are beet red."

Sunny glanced over her shoulder. Locals who knew her and her parents were watching, curious to see if there would be DeStefano family fireworks. Both of her parents sat with their heads bent, eating in silence.

Yep, Dad's ears were red. And if he had

another heart attack, it would be her fault.

Sunny turned back to her food as the anger within dimmed. She was acting like a child. If she wanted her parents to treat her like an adult, she had to act like one. This was between her and her mother. The sooner they settled it the better. "Excuse me." Sunny picked up her plate and glass and walked to her parents' booth. "May I join you?"

Betty Sue slid across the banquette to make room.

Sunny set down her food at the head of the table and pulled over an empty chair. "I don't want to take sides," she announced as she sat down.

"Fine way to behave," Betty Sue scolded under her breath.

"Employee or daughter. Pick one." Sunny ate another mouthful of pie.

"Employee," Vince said without looking up. "Costs less."

"Vince!" Betty Sue slapped his arm.

He continued eating his salad.

Sunny sighed. For better or worse, they were her parents. She couldn't help loving them, even if they did drive her nuts. "I vote daughter." Sunny set down her fork and looked at Betty Sue. "I need a mom, not a manager."

Betty Sue's chin trembled.

Sunny reached for her mother's hand. "Admit it. You've been having just as hard a time as I have."

Betty Sue's glance shot to Vince. She

nodded.

Sunny smiled. "Now that you're back for good, you don't need me to manage."

"Back for good?" Vince's head shot up.

Sunny nudged Betty Sue's arm. "Don't you think it's time to tell Dad you hate Florida? You've told everyone else."

Vince glared at his wife. "Is that true?"

Betty Sue opened her mouth but nothing came out. She tried again. "The sun is terrible for my skin," she said finally. "And I don't swim."

"Who's making you swim?" Vince sputtered.

"Sitting by the pool is a complete waste of time," Betty Sue continued, her words gaining momentum. "And the beach! There's sand everywhere."

"I wouldn't know," Sunny said. "We never went on vacation."

"Yes, we did," Betty Sue snapped. "Just not to the beach because I hate it."

Vince pressed a hand to his forehead. "Betty Sue," he said finally, "why did you agree to move to Florida?"

"Your heart," she said weakly. "You wanted to retire."

His gaze softened. "But you didn't."

Betty Sue shook her head.

Mission accomplished. Sunny finished the last bite of her pie. "You can go back to managing the Up Do. I can coordinate activities at Mountain Mist. And Dad can?" She shot her father a questioning look.

He picked up his fork. "Hire movers to bring our stuff back from Florida."

~

Buck forced his eyes wide, stared at the digital clock illuminating the dashboard. Three-fifteen a.m. He fixed his gaze once more on the tail lights of Carly Day's white car, alone on the road in front of him.

He'd tried to convince Carly Day to wait until daylight before leaving, but there was no talking her out of driving south. She was used to working nights, she'd insisted, and had slept on the flight from Vegas. At least he'd gotten her to agree to take Gina to dinner while he'd packed up his car. He'd debated calling Reo, but after what she'd said about their mother at the MacPhee house, he wasn't sure he should. He sent her a text explaining what was happening. When she didn't answer, he went to the restaurant. Gina and Carly Day were eager to leave. His mother drove fast, averaging over eighty miles an hour as she led him down the desolate highway.

Seeing Gina in awe of their mother didn't help his sour mood. His sister was eating up the fake kindness Carly Day lavished on her daughter. Had Buck neglected Gina so much she craved attention from the last person she should accept it from? Buck had a hard time believing Carly Day was trying to make up for rejecting Gina in Vegas and not calling afterwards. And even if their mother did feel guilty, that didn't mean she'd changed.

Images of the past few days flashed in his mind. Casting flies at garden gnomes. Pushing his way through the crowded Main Street sidewalk toward the flashing emergency lights. Hauling water-soaked salon furniture into the MacPhee house.

Kissing Sunny. His chest tightened as he thought of holding Sunny close, knowing that in that moment she'd wanted him as much as he'd wanted her. What was he doing, driving all night to New Orleans? He should be with Sunny. Holding her. Loving her.

He was in love with Sunny DeStefano.

And now that he finally gave the emotion a name, his heart ached with regret, because a relationship with Sunny would never work. No matter what she said about not caring about her mother's opinion, Sunny's family was important to her. Everybody could see that. He gulped, remembering how Sunny had chosen him over her parents. How would the evening have turned out if Carly Day hadn't shown up? Would Sunny have gone off with him just to spite her mother? Just thinking about the damage her choice could have done to her relationship with her parents made his head spin.

He stiffened his spine. No. He needed to be realistic. Sunny's life was in Lilac and his was a thousand miles away at the mouth of the Mississippi River. It was the same reason he'd had to be firm with Norbert. He hadn't meant to hurt his grandfather's feelings, but they had to be practical. Norbert needed to stay at Mountain Mist where he was safe, where all his needs were met. Buck didn't know the first thing about caring for someone who was elderly.

The lights of the Birmingham skyline loomed in the distance. Up ahead, Carly Day signaled to get off at a truck stop. Good, more coffee. Buck parked beside the white car and followed Carly Day and Gina inside. After freshening up, they met by the food court.

Carly Day studied the culinary options and laughed. "Can't decide if I want dinner or breakfast." She slipped her arm around Gina's shoulders. "Burgers or waffles? It's your birthday."

Buck cringed. He'd completely forgotten it was Gina's birthday. He watched as Carly Day and Gina headed for the breakfast counter, the click-clack of high heels echoing through the cavernous truck stop. He turned in the opposite direction, purchased a burger and the largest cup of coffee they sold, and made his way to their table.

Two men he presumed to be the drivers of the massive rigs parked in the lot, sat a couple tables away. One of the men stared openly at Carly Day and Gina as if he hadn't seen women in a year. Buck scowled at him until he looked away then stared at his wrapped burger, his appetite gone. The sterile neon-lit food court had him yearning suddenly for the Mountain Mist dining room or the homey atmosphere of The Shoebox. He wouldn't even have minded

Lulu's chattering.

Gina's face lit with delight as she dug into her whipped-cream-topped Belgian waffle. "Mom says we only have a few more hours to go."

He tilted his head. "You've driven this way before?"

Carly Day sipped her coffee. "Long time ago."

"With Norel Quisenbury?" he asked.

He watched her long eyelashes fly upward at the sound of Spike's given name then settle down, shielding her gaze. She sipped her coffee and seemed interested only in watching Gina eat.

Buck's irritation swelled. "Why didn't you tell me that my grandparents owned an orchard outside Lilac? Or that I was born in a trailer?"

Gina's fork froze half way to her mouth. "You were born in a trailer?"

Carly Day's perfectly made-up features stiffened. "Spike's parents knew about you. You can't blame me if they didn't reach out."

"Did you know he died in prison?" Buck asked.

"No, I didn't." Carly Day set down her cup, her tone cool. "I'm not surprised."

Bile burned the back of his throat. "You're never responsible for anything, are you? You blow in and out of people's lives and hit the road when things get boring. What happened in Vegas? Did that kid you were dating get wise and figure out your real age?" He crumpled his food wrappers and shoved them into the bag. "For God's sake, Gina, do not go with her. Come home with me."

Gina's wide-eyed gaze moved between her mother and her brother. Confusion warred with denial on her delicate features.

Please, God, let Gina make the right choice. Not that living with him was necessarily the best choice. He knew he hadn't given his sister the guidance she'd needed. He'd been so preoccupied in his own affairs, he'd only looked up and noticed when Gina had gotten into trouble. Even then, it was only to fix the immediate problem instead of offering her meaningful guidance. If only he had the chance to do it again. He felt like he was missing something, that there were words he could say to change Gina's mind. For the life of him, he didn't know what they were. He'd give anything to have Sunny here right now, consoling Gina the way she had after the car accident. Sunny would know what to do.

Carly Day patted Gina's hand and flashed her an engaging smile. "Finish your food, sweetheart. Then we'll go."

Buck's heart sank as Gina swallowed the last of her waffle and nodded. He watched, defeated, as Carly Day hurried her daughter out the door.

"Wait!" He raced to catch up with them as they approached the car. He gripped Gina's shoulders, studied her face beneath the street lamp. "I'm sorry I wasn't there when you needed me. I'm making you a promise. If you need anything—and I mean anything—call me and I'll be there. No questions asked."

Gina nodded and threw her arms around him. "I love you," she whispered.

Buck blinked. She'd never told him that before. "I love you, too." He pressed her head to his shoulder and looked at Carly Day. "Take care of her, or you'll be hearing from me."

She arched an eyebrow at him. "Of course." She climbed into the car.

The highway filled with Saturday morning traffic as they neared New Orleans. It didn't surprise him one bit that his mother didn't stop again. She wasn't going to give Buck another chance to change Gina's mind. He watched with sadness as her white convertible merged onto a downtown expressway. He swallowed the lump in his throat and drove until he reached his own exit ramp. At least he'd gotten Gina to promise to call him if she needed anything.

He cruised the winding road to the backwoods dock that was the home of his tour boat company. The *Easy Does It* was tied up at the peer, gently bobbing in the water. He parked Cole next to his battered Jeep, his limbs aching as he climbed out and stretched. Twenty steps up the exterior staircase and he'd be in his apartment above the office, free to collapse into oblivion.

Remy emerged from the office, his Easy Does It Eco-Tours baseball cap shielding his eyes from the bright sun. He shook Buck's hand. "Didn't expect you back today. Good trip?"

"We drove straight through." Buck stifled a yawn as he surveyed the dock and property. As far as he could tell, everything appeared to be in order.

"We?" Remy looked around. "Where's Gina?"

Buck shook his head, exhaustion overcoming him. "She rode separately with our mother. They went to New Orleans." He headed for the staircase.

"I know you're tired," Remy said, his voice hesitant, "but have you had a chance to read our proposal?"

Buck nodded. "Got a couple questions."

"You're considering it?" Remy's face lit with excitement.

Buck studied the hard-working young man standing before him. Remy was his trusted boat captain, competent and reliable. Could Gina have driven Remy away with her constant flirting? Conversely, would it have been that awkward if Gina and Remy had started dating? Buck had interfered and look where his sister was now, gallivanting off with Carly Day to grow up fast working in casinos.

Remy was a good guy. Buck was a fool.

~

Bright and early on Monday morning, Sunny sat with her father on the front porch of the MacPhee house tying flies. The clang of hammers and whir of power tools punctuated the quiet morning air. Betty Sue hurried along the front walk, speaking rapidly into her phone and motioning to the delivery men to follow her up the porch steps.

Vince sighed. "I'll never get her out of Lilac now."

Betty Sue stuck her head out the door. "Should the styling station mirrors be flush to the counters or raised eight inches?"

Before Sunny or Vince could answer, she spun away. "Never mind." She disappeared inside.

Sunny squinted at the tiny wisp of feather she'd woven beneath the wire and gave it a snip. "Mom hated Florida that much?"

"Never gave it a chance. When your Uncle Steve and I went golfing, your Aunt Patty took Betty Sue around to meet her friends at the pool." He shrugged. "After a couple outings, Betty Sue made excuses and begged off. Started spending her days on the phone and on the Internet, communicating with everybody back here."

"That mirror is not centered. Take it down and do it again," Betty Sue commanded, her voice carrying through the open windows.

Sunny shook her head. Those poor workers. Did they know what they were getting into when they signed a contract to complete the renovations in ninety days? "Think you'll ever go back?"

Vince removed the finished hook from the vice and set it gently into Sunny's case. "For vacation once a year, if I can pry your mother away."

"I'm here, Betty Sue. Hang up." Lavinia scurried up the walk on rhinestone-studded stilettos, panting as she spoke into her phone. She paused at the top step to catch her breath. "Betty Sue needs my opinion on the display case." She smoothed her skirt, yanked open the screen door, and hurried inside.

Sunny wound the loose thread around a spool and stored it in her case. "What makes you think Mom will take vacations now? She never did before."

Vince winked at her. "She would if she had a manager here she could trust."

"Then Mom needs to talk to Nadine. I'll cut hair at Mountain Mist. That's it." Sunny had sat up talking with her parents until after midnight their first night back. They hadn't liked everything Sunny had said about the difficulties of being a daughter and an employee. She wasn't sure they'd believed everything she'd said about Buck and Gina, but frankly she no longer cared. She'd gotten everything off her chest. In some odd way, Betty Sue seemed as relieved as Sunny that they wouldn't be working together anymore.

"Vince, come in here, please," Betty Sue called. "We need your opinion."

Vince patted Sunny's arm. "Well, you can always change your mind." He sauntered into the house.

Those two. She loved them and wanted

marriage and a family of her own because of them. But running a hair salon was their dream, not hers. Why had it taken her so long to figure that out? One thing she knew for sure. She wouldn't miss all the hair salon gossip. It had always made her uncomfortable. What she hadn't fully understood was its impact. Whispered gossip could hurt as much as a slap. Buck had helped her to see that.

And now he was gone. She closed her eyes, reliving the feel of his lips on hers. Had it been too much for him, having a crowd cheering them on when he was so private about his emotions? She hadn't heard a word from him in over a week. Maybe that was her answer.

Really, God? I had to fall in love with a man who doesn't like attention and doesn't believe in marriage? She knew in her heart that God wanted what was best for everyone. Did that mean she and Buck had a future together, or that she had to let him go?

Her phone on the table buzzed. A text from Reo. *You need to tell Buck.*

She tapped the screen. *We've been over that. Let me.*

No. You promised.

How about if Jack tells him?

No!

Dinner tonight? Jack has class.

Sure. What time?

Six. I'm craving Lulu's meatloaf.

Me, too, and I'm not expecting. Sunny set down her phone. Her dad had survived a heart attack. Her mother was taking over the Up Do. She had friends, a new job, so much to be grateful for. She needed to focus on that, not on her broken heart.

Vince returned to the porch just as she finished packing away her fly-tying supplies. "I'm heading over to Mountain Mist," she said. "Want to come along?"

"Meeting Donnie for lunch. Finalizing the details of our fishing trip."

"Fishing trip?" she frowned. "I'm surprised Leanne is letting Donnie go anywhere without her. The honeymoon's barely over."

"Wonders never cease." He chuckled as he bent down to kiss Sunny's cheek. "Have fun. Hey, Tanya."

Sunny looked up to see Tanya Lee scurrying up the walk. She'd gone blond the week before. Dressed in a jungle print sundress with a matching green purse and stilettos, she clutched a piece of paper. It flapped in the breeze like a battle flag.

Oh, my. Had Tanya finally found the perfect hairstyle? Sunny smiled to herself. Betty Sue would have fun with this.

"Just the people I want to see. Where's Betty Sue?" Tanya demanded.

Vince inclined his head toward the screen door. "Inside."

"Betty Sue," Tanya shouted over the drilling noise. "Come out here."

Sunny straightened. What was all this about? She hadn't seen Tanya this excited since the settlement check from the insurance company arrived.

Betty Sue emerged from the house with Lavinia in tow.

"Ready, everybody? Look at this." Tanya held up the flyer like a first-grader showing off her art work.

"Tanya's Closet," Sunny read. A consignment shop ad? She scanned the details. "That's the old salon address."

Betty Sue studied the flyer. "Vince and I were just talking about what to do with that space."

"I got the idea last night driving home from Charlottesville. By the way, Sunny, I saw the cutest robin's egg blue dress that would look perfect with your hair." She cleared her throat. "Anyway, that's when I got the idea. The old salon would be perfect for a consignment shop. What do you think?"

Betty Sue's brow furrowed. "You want to change the old salon into a consignment shop?"

Vince nodded. "Makes sense. You can take out a lease. What do you say, Betty Sue?"

Lavinia clutched Betty Sue's arm. "Oh, let her, Betty Sue. Just think, we can meet there and shop between hair appointments."

"On second thought." Vince chuckled as he kissed Betty Sue's cheek. "Whatever you decide is fine with me. See you for dinner."

Betty Sue turned to Sunny. "What do you think about this?"

Sunny shrugged. "Sounds good to me."

"Woohoo!" Tanya gripped Sunny's hand. "I was hoping you and Gina might help me get it set up. After all, it was Gina's idea."

"The consignment shop was Gina's idea?" Betty Sue's jaw dropped.

Tanya nodded. "She brought up consignment shops when she was working at the salon. She has a great sense of style. Did I tell you she came over to the house a couple times and helped me organize my closets?" Tanya tossed her curls and pointed at her hair. "And she recommended this cut."

"Gina?" Betty Sue's eyes flew wide. She gave Sunny a questioning look.

"She's a natural when it comes to hair and clothes." Sunny snapped her supply case shut. "She's gone to New Orleans."

"New Orleans? When is she coming back?" Tanya asked.

Sunny nibbled her lip. "I don't know."

Chapter Nine

Buck finished sweeping the dock and leaned on the broom handle. The early morning sun peeking through the cypress trees promised another sweltering day. The humid air seemed to rise up from the ground itself and hover over the flat terrain. No mountain breezes here.

He'd swept the Mountain Mist salon after his first visit, swept the Up Do after the flood. Unfortunately, for all his attempts to help clean up, he'd only made things worse. Pushing Gina to rebel. Disrupting Norbert's peaceful life. Driving a wedge between Sunny and her mother. Messes that wouldn't have happened if he'd left town as he'd originally planned. Messes he didn't know how to fix.

He'd called Norbert the day he'd arrived back at the dock, letting him know he and Gina had left Lilac. Norbert had sounded resigned, his voice barely audible when he said goodbye. At least he'd answered the phone. Gina wouldn't reply to any of his texts or voice mail messages. And Sunny?

He couldn't get her out of his thoughts. The

way she smiled when he made a joke. Her kindness with Norbert and the Mountain Mist residents. Her patience with Gina. But the image of her walking that labyrinth, lost in thought and so at peace, haunted him the most. He'd walked the labyrinth himself that day, self-consciously looking over his shoulder every other minute to see if anyone was watching. Sunny had walked it with total freedom, confident in her purpose, not caring one bit who watched or passed judgement.

The same way she'd wrapped her arms around his neck and pulled his head down to kiss him in front of all those Mountain Mist residents.

He closed his eyes, conjuring the feeling of her slender body in his arms, the taste of her lips so soft on his. He thought staying away might lessen the pain of longing, but it had only gotten worse. She needed to work things out with her family. He had no right to get into the middle of that. Besides, what could he say if he called? That he'd left because taking care of his sister and his business was more important than her?

A horn beeped. He opened his eyes and raised his hand in acknowledgment. A small white bus came to a stop by the dock. Father Lou's retreatants, right on time. Buck smiled at the quaint terminology the old New Orleans priest had used the night before when he'd called to make the last minute request. A group of men on retreat wanted to tour the swamp, see the splendor of God's creation. Buck had tried to refuse, explaining he'd given his entire crew time off to attend a friend's wedding, but Father Lou had persisted. The men had traveled a long way. They wouldn't be any trouble. Buck should be able to handle the small group all by himself. In the end, he had given in.

A window popped open. "Is this Easy Does It Eco Tours?" the bus driver called out.

Buck squinted into the sun. "Donnie?" He threw down the broom and hurried across the lot.

Donnie's smiling face disappeared inside the window as Buck ran to the bus. Donnie met him at the bottom steps and pulled him into a hug.

Buck's heart felt like it would jump right out of his chest. "What are you doing here? Is something wrong?"

"Nothing's wrong." Donnie jerked a thumb over his shoulder. "Somebody had to drive the bus for these guys."

"Guys?" Buck scanned the tinted windows, picked up the sound of men's laughter. "Is that..." His voice caught in the back of his throat.

"Step back. Gotta deploy the lift." Donnie disappeared into the bus.

Buck spun around as the large side door slid open.

Norbert and Harlan stood together on a platform. Norbert gripped his walker with one hand and elbowed Harlan with the other. "Told you I didn't need the chair."

Harlan shook his head and looked

heavenward as the platform lowered to the ground.

Buck pulled his grandfather close and hugged him tight. "What are you doing here?"

Norbert winked. "Old guy road trip."

"Maybe you don't need a chair," a voice called from inside the bus, "but Dad does. Stop bragging and get off the lift."

"Dewey?" Buck released his grandfather and shook Harlan's hand as the three stepped away from the platform.

"In the flesh." Harlan chuckled.

Dewey appeared on the lift beside Frank. Once the platform lowered to the ground, he rolled his father's chair forward to join the others. "Wow," he said, his voice filled with awe as he took in the boat dock and marsh grass. "You really do live in the swamp."

Buck shook hands with Dewey and Frank, his heartbeat kicking up a notch as he watched the bus door. Was there anyone else? His breath caught as the platform glided upward, his stomach churning as he waited to see who would emerge next.

The bus door slammed shut. His shoulders slumped. Of course, Sunny didn't come. What was he thinking?

"Good to see you again, Buck," a deep voice said.

Buck whirled around. Sunny's father stood next to Donnie, hand outstretched. "Mr. DeStefano!" Buck gripped his hand.

"Please. Vince." He smiled and looked

around, his gaze taking in the surroundings. "So, this is your tour boat company."

"Yes, sir." Buck drank in the smiling faces like a drowning man. He couldn't believe his eyes. What were they doing here? "Want to look around?"

Donnie leaned close. "Uh, that's kinda why we came."

Harlan nudged Norbert. "You're gonna need the chair for this."

Norbert gave an exasperated sigh. "Fine."

"I'm on it." Dewey disappeared inside the bus and emerged a moment later with a folded wheelchair. He snapped it open with one quick motion and held it while Norbert sat. "I'm getting really good at this," he said to Buck over his shoulder.

"I can tell." Buck pushed Norbert's chair and led the way to the office, grateful he'd paved the gravel with blacktop and added wheelchair ramps the prior spring. "My apartment's up there." He pointed to the exterior staircase. "Kind of a mess, but you're welcome to look."

Donnie looked at Norbert and Frank. "I think we can all imagine what a bachelor pad looks like, right guys?"

"I wanna see." Dewey parked Frank's chair next to Norbert's, ran up the steps, and threw open the door.

Buck cringed. Dirty dishes. Unmade bed. Pile of laundry.

Dewey whistled. "Fifty-inch flat screen and

a water view," he called down.

The men nodded in appreciation. Dewey ran down the steps and slapped Buck on the back. "Nice digs."

Buck led them to his office. "This is where I meet with clients, order supplies, set up the schedules." The men filed in, drawn immediately to the wall covered with nautical maps.

"This one's over a hundred years old," Harlan said, his tone impressed.

"That's right, you're the Lilac town archivist." Buck pulled open a map drawer. "Here are some others you might like."

Vince studied a collage of smiling faces filling the Happy Customers display. "There must be two hundred pictures here. Did you take all of these?"

Buck shook his head. "We invite visitors to send us their photographs. We also ask permission to print and hang photos they post on social media."

"Nothing like happy clients to promote a business. Lots of repeats, I see." Vince pointed out families that had made visiting the swamp an annual outing.

"Look at the alligator," Dewey eased Frank's wheelchair closer to a set of framed wildlife photos. Dewey glanced at Buck. "You took these nature shots?"

Buck nodded, embarrassed and proud at the same time. Photography had been a necessity, at first, to promote the business. Over time, it had become Buck's way of capturing the natural wonders he saw every day.

Donnie studied the framed picture hanging behind the desk. "Your crew?"

"Great bunch of guys." Buck suddenly wished his crew members were here so everyone could meet. "Most of them grew up on the water. Got family who live along the bayou. They watch out for each other. Kind of like living in Lilac," Buck added. He'd never thought of that before. The residents of the bayou knew each other's histories, the good and the bad, and took care of each other. Just like the residents of any small town.

Dewey looked up from his conversation with Frank and grinned. "Don't know about you fellas, but I'm ready to feed some alligators."

"Sorry, but no feeding the animals," Buck explained as he led the way outside. "We do eco tours."

"What's that mean?" Dewey asked.

"It means we try to leave the swamp the way we found it. Use smaller boats with quieter engines. No tempting the wildlife with food and no fishing." Buck stopped at the dock where *Easy Does It*, a twenty-passenger boat, and *Easy Does It Again*, a six-passenger skiff, floated in the water. The skiff would be more fun, allowing them to maneuver into backwaters the larger boat couldn't enter. However, the *Easy Does It*, with its canopy and cushioned seats, would be more accessible for Norbert and Frank. He headed for the larger boat. "Hold onto your hats and get out the sun screen," he announced in his tour boat guide voice. "You're about to see Honey Island Swamp, one of the most untouched wetlands in Louisiana."

After everyone settled into their seats, he started the engine. "Can't promise you'll see alligators, but keep your eyes open for egrets and feral hogs."

Buck brought the boat up to twenty knots as they cruised the outer bayou then reduced the speed to a crawl as they entered the inner swamp. The expressions of awe on everyone's faces reminded him of his first visit.

"Amazing," Vince said.

Donnie jumped to his feet and pointed into the air. "Is that a bald eagle?"

Buck nodded. "The nest is up around the bend."

They watched the majestic bird in silence until it disappeared from view.

"Looks like a pirate movie," Dewey observed as they passed an old fishing cabin nestled beneath moss-draped Cyprus trees.

"I don't know about pirate movies, but there've been a bunch of wildlife documentaries filmed here." Buck wiped his brow. "Hey, Dewey, pass out some water bottles. They're in the cooler."

Before the sun made the heat and humidity unbearable, Buck turned the boat around and headed back to the dock. Once on dry land, Donnie and Vince got the gas grill going as the men settled around the picnic table in the shade.

"Another nice thing about running a business with a concession stand," Buck said as he set a platter of hamburgers and potato salad on the table. "Always food around." Buck took a seat on the bench next to his grandfather. "What made you decide to come fishing down here?"

The men all looked at each other. "Well," Vince began, breaking the silence. "Donnie and I have been fishing buddies for over forty years. When I heard he was taking a fishing trip, I invited myself along."

"Uh-huh." Buck nodded

Dewey set down his can of soda. "When Donnie mentioned he was organizing the trip, I asked if we could come."

"Father Lou said you were on retreat," Buck said, confused.

All eyes turned to Donnie. "We were. Father Dominic arranged for us to stay with Father Lou after Harlan asked him to let us borrow the bus."

"Father Dominic?" Buck looked up. Sure enough, the side of the bus said St. Andrews. He hadn't even noticed.

Harlan turned to Norbert. "You gonna make me say it?"

Norbert stared at his plate while he chewed his hamburger.

Buck stiffened. "Say what?"

Norbert set down his hamburger and faced his grandson. "I shouldn't have asked you to move me back to the orchard. I need to live at Mountain Mist because of my health. Didn't mean to drive you away with my silly notions."

Buck's thoughts spun as the air whooshed out of his lungs. No wonder Norbert had sounded so distant on the phone. He gripped his grandfather's shoulder. "You thought I was mad because you wanted to live with me at the orchard? That was one of the best things anyone has ever asked me. A shock, but still, one of the best."

Norbert blinked. "Then why did you leave?"

A yellow-throated warbler sounded in the distance. Buck scanned the circle of expectant faces. The overwhelming urge to jump to his feet and escape to his office seized him. He should tell them he had to go to a meeting. He should say he had to make a call. He gripped the bench, fighting the wave of discomfort assaulting him. Fear of scrutiny. Aversion to pity. Shame for his parents' behavior. The ghosts of past embarrassments pounded him.

And yet.

Something in these men's eyes, their open, non-judgmental expressions, quietly assured him, revealed the power of the truth confronting him. Men who'd known him since he was a kid, who'd heard all the gossip about his family, had traveled hundreds of miles to help their elderly friend reconcile with the grandson who'd broken his heart.

Buck eased his grip on the bench. He wasn't running away this time. He glanced at Vince. "You didn't tell them?"

"Tell us what?" Dewey asked.

At Vince's smile of encouragement, Buck took a deep breath. "Well, it kind of happened like this..."

~

"I'm not sure this was a good idea," Sunny said as she waited outside the New Orleans casino employee entrance early on Saturday morning. "Gina's going to be exhausted."

"That's the whole point," Tanya said, taking a bite of her beignet. "Oh, my goodness, I could so live here. The music. The food. Maybe I should move."

"Wouldn't that defeat the purpose of our visit?" Sunny asked, stifling a yawn. She should have her head examined for agreeing to take the predawn flight.

"Oh, yeah, right." Tanya swallowed the last bite of her beignet and licked her fingers.

Sunny couldn't believe she'd let Tanya talk her into this scheme. Yesterday evening she'd been enjoying a perfectly fine dinner with her mother when Tanya had burst in with her plan. Fly to New Orleans. Surprise Gina. Bring her back to Lilac. "You realize she may not want to come with us."

"Of course, she will. Didn't you hear what Reo said? Gina works night shift in the kitchen. They won't let her wait tables until she's twenty-one."

"What if Gina likes working in the kitchen? Maybe she's made friends. Maybe she has a boyfriend," Sunny said. Maybe Buck had finally put aside his protests and Gina was dating

Remy.

"Doubt it. Hard to make friends or date when you're working nights. Trust me. I've had firsthand experience."

"Working in a casino is not the same as working at a truck stop," Sunny said.

Tanya sniffed. "I wouldn't be so sure about that. Besides I'm giving Gina a job *and* a free place to stay. She has an incredible sense of style plus she speaks Spanish. I need her help to get Tanya's Closet off the ground."

Sunny sipped her coffee. She didn't want to get Tanya's hopes up. She'd seen the look on Gina's face when she'd left with Carly Day. So excited, so happy to finally be with her mother. What right did they have to take Gina away from her mom after they'd lived so many years apart?

Sunny looked up and down the alley. A steady stream of employees were arriving for the day shift. Gina should be coming out of the casino any minute.

"Sunny! Tanya! What are you doing here?" a voice exclaimed.

Sunny spun around.

Gina stood behind them, an expression of shock on her face. Her hair was neatly pinned up, her kitchen uniform spotless. Her eyes sparkled with surprise as she threw her arms around them.

"We came to rescue you," Tanya announced, laughing.

Gina's gaze shot back and forth between

them, her smile disappearing. "I'm confused."

Employees exited the casino, their steps slow, their shoulders slumped after a long night's work. Compared to them, Gina looked like she could star in a cereal commercial. "When did you start working days?" Sunny asked.

"You work days?" Tanya said, as if she'd just noticed how bright and perky Gina looked. "Reo said you worked nights."

"I do. I volunteered for an extra shift on my day off to make more money." Gina looked towards the entrance. "It's great seeing you guys. Do you want to meet when I get off?"

"Get off? I want you to quit," Tanya said. "I need you to help manage Tanya's Closet."

"I already helped you clean your closet," Gina replied. "Did you mess it up again?"

"Tanya is opening a consignment shop in the old Up Do salon space called Tanya's Closet," Sunny explained. "The new Up Do will be opening in the MacPhee house next door."

Gina's jaw dropped. "You want me to help manage a consignment shop? I don't know how to be a manager."

"You know plenty. You'll be great," Tanya assured her.

"Would you rather stay here with your mom?" Sunny asked softly, ignoring Tanya's scowl. Better to talk about this now than have Gina later regret leaving her mother.

Gina's expression crumbled.

Uh-oh, here it comes. Sunny was suddenly

glad she'd come along. Tanya was going to be crushed by Gina's refusal.

"Oh, Sunny," Gina cried, throwing her arms around Sunny's neck. "Mom leaves for work when I get home. We never spend any time together. I don't even know where she's been the past three days."

Sunny held Gina close, patting her back. "It's okay," she whispered, ignoring the curious stares of passing employees.

"I love to cook, but I hate working in the casino kitchen," Gina wailed. "Is that stupid? Maybe I should have accepted Buck's offer to go to culinary school instead."

"It's not stupid," Sunny assured, her heart easing with the knowledge that Buck had encouraged his sister and offered her a path to a future career.

"That's it," Tanya exclaimed. She drained her coffee cup and tossed it into a nearby recycle bin. "Life is too short to spend it doing something you hate. Believe me. I worked six thankless years in a truck stop."

Gina released Sunny, her expression stricken.

"We will drive you to Buck's house if you want to enroll in culinary school," Tanya continued in a no-nonsense tone. "Or you can return to Lilac and help me manage Tanya's Closet. Is there another option I don't know about?"

Gina thought a minute. She shook her head.

Just show up at Buck's house? After he'd

left and then hadn't called her? Sunny stiffened her spine. No time to be a coward. If returning to Buck was what Gina wanted to do, then that's what they'd do. It didn't matter how awkward it might make her feel. Gina's future was at stake. She squeezed Gina's shoulders. "What do you want to do?"

"If you come work for me," Tanya said, giving Gina a serious look. "I need you to make a one-year commitment. Can you do that?"

Sunny held her breath while Gina stared at the ground.

"I don't know," Gina said.

~

"Oh, man. Awesome," Dewey exclaimed as multicolored slot machine lights flashed and electronic chimes dinged around them.

Buck rolled his eyes. "First time?"

"Don't judge me." Dewey drank it in, eyes alight, like a kid at a carnival.

"Don't make me regret bringing you." Buck pushed past the rows of slot machines and through the Saturday afternoon crowd. Donnie, Norbert, and the rest of the men were two blocks away, enjoying a late lunch at a seafood restaurant overlooking the Mississippi River. They'd understood completely when he'd said he needed to find Gina and make sure she was all right. It didn't matter that she hadn't answered his calls or replied to his texts. He'd be darned if he gave up on her. The men of Lilac hadn't given up on him.

"Hey, that guy just won five hundred

bucks," Dewey said, pointing at a man pumping his fist in the air and shouting.

"Probably spent a thousand dollars doing it," Buck shot back. Maybe bringing Dewey as his wingman hadn't been the best idea. Things could get awkward fast once he found Gina.

First, he had to find Carly Day.

He headed for the gaming tables. Sure enough, there she was, surrounded by a circle of men, dealing blackjack. She wore a crisp white shirt and black vest, her blond hair falling in waves to her shoulders. She flipped the cards expertly, smiling pleasantly, naming the cards as they fell.

He stood outside the circle of players, watching.

"That's your mom?" Dewey whispered.

Buck heard the undertone of surprise and ignored it. Carly Day had perfected the art of looking young.

He didn't have to wait long for her to notice him. Within minutes, a replacement dealer arrived. How did she do that? A buzzer under the table? A silent look exchanged with a staff member? Without a word, Carly Day rose and walked towards the casino lobby.

"Where's she going?" Dewey asked.

"Come on." Buck followed her across the lobby into an atrium filled with tropical trees and exotic plants. Guests milled about sipping drinks and chatting. Colorful birds flew overhead. Dewey waited off to the side as Buck approached his mother.

Carly Day stood just beyond a soaring water fountain. "I'm on a break. Ten minutes." She glanced impatiently at her cell phone.

"Where's Gina?" Buck asked.

"She left." Carly Day slipped her phone into her pocket.

Left the casino? His stomach sank. "Where did she go?"

"Back to Lilac."

His heart jolted. "When? With whom?"

"This morning. Some girl named Tanya wants to give her a job."

Tanya? He motioned Dewey over. "Do you know Tanya? She came and took Gina back to Lilac."

Dewey looked confused, then his expression brightened. "Must be Tanya Lee. She's been living large since receiving that insurance settlement."

"She wants Gina to work for her." Carly Day studied Dewey's face. "Are you related to Frank Deutsch?"

Dewey nodded. "He's my dad."

She smiled. "Tell him Carly Day says hi." She turned to Buck. "You can thank me later for making sure Gina hated working here."

"What's that supposed to mean?" he asked, warily. He'd always figured his mom must've developed some keen survival skills to live the life she'd chosen. Did those skills include manipulating her teenage daughter?

"I told the kitchen manager to give Gina the night shift. It's the worst." Her wrinkled nose made it look like she spoke from experience.

He imagined Gina, exhausted and lonely, toiling long hours in a stifling hot kitchen, sweat streaming down her face. "Why? Did having a daughter around cramp your social life?" he asked, unable to keep the sarcasm out of his voice.

Dewey's eyes shot wide. Without a word he fled to the other side of the atrium.

Carly Day's cheeks reddened. "I was wrong to say what I did in Vegas." She looked down. "You don't know how many times I've wished I could take it back."

His mother's stinging words—*If anybody asks, say I'm your aunt*—had emotionally destroyed Gina. He suddenly realized how much courage it had taken for his sister to ask Carly Day for help. He felt ashamed. He should have paid more attention, listened more closely when Gina had said she wanted to return to New Orleans.

Carly Day lifted her gaze to his. "Just because Lilac never worked for me doesn't mean it won't work for her."

Buck froze at the sound of his own words coming from his mother's lips. He'd thought the same thing when he'd returned for Donnie's wedding. "You didn't quit your Vegas job, did you?"

Her blue eyes flashed. "No. But I'll be quitting this one tonight."

"I suppose I should thank you," he said, his voice stiff.

She pressed a hand to her throat, suddenly appearing flustered. "Considering this is..." her voice choked. She shook her head and took a deep breath, appearing to fight for composure "Considering this is the first time one of my children has asked me for help, it's the least I could do."

In that instant, Buck saw his mother as she really was. A restless spirit who carried her burdens alone, moving from place to place, never satisfied. He didn't understand her choices, but he no longer hated her for them. For all her self-confidence, she was fragile, vulnerable, like everyone else.

He slipped his arms gently around her shoulders. She stood stiffly in the circle of his awkward embrace, the same way he had stood when Sunny surprised him with a hug. He'd lacked the confidence to hug Sunny back because he'd believed he didn't deserve her affection. What Sunny couldn't have known that day, but what he knew now, was that the hug had mattered even if he'd been too ashamed to respond. "It's okay if you don't hug me back," he whispered.

Carly Day collapsed against him, her hands clutching his shirt, her sobs muffled against his chest. "I'm sorry," she whispered, gulping for air, as if she were drowning in the depths of an emotional sea. She stepped backward, wiping at her face to compose herself. "I've got to go."

He didn't want her to leave. "You're quitting," he protested, his voice barely above a croak. "Come with us."

She shook her head.

Buck closed his eyes, tried to get his feelings under control. Carly Day had her own life, her own secrets. Maybe one day she'd share them with him.

He held out his hand. "Give me your phone. I'm putting my number in it."

She pulled her phone from her pocket and handed it to him.

He quickly entered his number in her contact list and sent his phone a text. "Answer when I call you," he said as he returned her phone.

Her lips quivered. "I will." She tucked it back into her pocket.

He watched in silence as she walked away. He may never understand her. He may never be able to depend on her. For better or worse, they were linked, mother and son, no matter what had happened in the past, no matter what happened in the future.

"You okay?" Dewey asked.

Buck nodded, afraid that if he spoke, he'd be drowning in the same emotional tide his mother had just barely survived.

Chapter Ten

On Monday afternoon, Sunny sat along the sidelines of the Mountain Mist bocce ball court. Mr. Zignetti and Colonel Collins stood nose to nose.

"My ball was closer—until you nudged it with your foot," Mr. Zignetti shouted.

"I did not touch your ball," Colonel Collins replied, chin in the air, his tone haughty.

Sunny rolled her eyes. In the past, when she'd only come around for haircuts, everyone must have been on their best behavior. Now, as activities coordinator, she got to see everyone's competitive side. The gloves came off. No holds barred. Didn't matter if it was checkers, bocce ball, or fly fishing.

The image of Buck practicing his casting with that silly garden gnome brought a rush of moisture to her eyes. She clenched her fists. She was not going to cry again. Every corner of Mountain Mist reminded her of him. The hair salon. The dining room. Norbert's face. She'd nearly lost it the first time she'd seen Norbert after Buck had left, he looked so pale and withdrawn. Thank goodness, Dewey and Frank had invited Norbert along on their fishing trip.

Mr. Zignetti kicked the grass. "Contemptible miscreant!"

Colonel Collins shook his fist. "Desperate hooligan."

Mrs. Skokel maneuvered her wheelchair to the bench where Sunny sat. "Perhaps you should intervene, dear, before someone has a stroke?"

Sunny shook her head. "Best to get it out now. Otherwise they'll ruin everyone's dinner."

She was done with holding in resentment. Clearing the air with her mother had been a messy emotional business. Now that they'd finally separated their personal lives from their work responsibilities, they were able to function as independent adults. Her mother was happy about opening the new salon and Sunny was happy to be working at Mountain Mist—even if every corner did remind her of Buck.

As Mrs. Skokel moved away, Dr. Dalir walked over and sat on the bench. "How are you going to settle this argument?" she asked, shielding her eyes with her hand.

"I'm thinking arm wrestling."

Dr. Dalir chuckled. "Have you thought any more about the online certificate program in Health Care Management?"

Sunny nibbled her lip. She'd never considered getting certified in any field that didn't have to do with the hair salon business. This was a big step away from how she'd envisioned her life would turn out. "Would I still be able to cut hair here at Mountain Mist?"

she asked.

"Of course." Dr. Dalir smiled. "You have a natural gift. Everyone here appreciates it. I know I do." She tossed her head, smiling as her short dark waves moved across her cheeks.

Sunny smiled in relief, praying she'd never take God's wonderful surprises for granted.

Dr. Dalir pointed. "That's odd. Doesn't the St. Andrew's bus usually come in the morning?"

Sunny glanced over at the small, white bus rounding the drive. It rolled to a stop next to the bocce ball court.

Donnie Greene waved at her from the driver's seat.

She waved back. Wait a minute. Donnie was on a fishing trip? Why was he driving the St. Andrew's bus?

Vince strolled down the bus steps.

"Dad!" She ran over and gave her father a hug. "I didn't know you'd taken the bus on your fishing trip."

Vince laughed and kissed her cheek. "Seemed like the best option for this crew."

The side door opened. Harlan and Dewey stood with Frank on the lift. They waved as the platform lowered them to the curb.

"Catch anything?" Sunny asked.

Dewey chuckled as he wheeled Frank's chair off the platform. "Oh, yeah."

Sunny glanced up and gasped. Buck stepped onto the lift, his dark gaze locked with hers. Her heart pounded at the base of her throat. Every fiber of her being tingled at the sight of him,

Norbert stood beside his grandson, barely leaning on his walker as the lift lowered them to the ground. He nudged Buck's arm. "Told you I didn't need the chair."

Buck walked slowly towards her. "Sunny, I—"

She held up her hand. "Excuse me." She marched over to Norbert and glared at him, hands on her hips. "Are you dying?"

~

Buck whirled around. "What?"

All conversation stopped. Out of the corner of his eye, Buck saw Colonel Collins, Mr. Zignetti, and Mrs. Skokel inch closer to the group, not wanting to miss a single word. Dr. Dalir and Harlan, who knew the ins and outs of everyone's lives, appeared stunned by Sunny's question.

Sunny locked her gaze on Norbert, undeterred by the circle of shocked faces staring at her. "You heard me." She crossed her arms and tapped her foot, waiting.

Buck stepped to her side. "What are you talking about?" he whispered.

"That day I was cutting hair, you asked me what was wrong," she said without turning her head. Her gaze stayed pinned on Norbert. "You're not dying, are you?"

Buck watched as his grandfather hung his head. "Aside from having two bum legs that don't move as fast as I'd like, no, I'm not dying," Norbert said finally.

Buck exhaled the breath he'd been holding.

The thought of losing Norbert now, after everything they'd been through, left him speechless.

Sunny's stern expression relaxed as she hugged the old man's shoulders. "Do you know how concerned I was?" she asked, her tone gentle.

"I'm sorry." Norbert lifted his gaze to hers, his expression sincere. "But I meant everything else I said."

"What else did you say?" Buck demanded.

"Never mind!" Sunny and Norbert answered in unison.

Buck's jaw dropped as everyone around him burst out laughing.

Vince clapped Donnie on the back. "Best fishing trip ever."

Donnie pulled Buck into a hug. "Let's make it an annual tradition."

Buck hugged him back. He was getting better at riding the waves of feelings instead of clenching up. And these men, with their selfless concern for him, had given him some emotional wallops.

"Next year, same time, same place. Right, Dad?" Dewey asked as he unloaded the Mountain Mist residents' gear from the bus storage compartment.

"You betcha," Frank said with a grin. "Right, Harlan?"

"Wouldn't miss it," Harlan replied, joining the other Mountain Mist residents as they walked towards the entrance.

Buck looked at Donnie and Vince, his heart full. "I don't know how to—"

Vince patted his shoulder. "Save it, son. She's almost at her car."

"What?" Buck spun around. Sunny! She was halfway across the parking lot. He shot a panicked glance at his grandfather.

Norbert chuckled. "You'd be a fool to let her get away."

Buck took off running, the men's laughter echoing behind him. How could she move so fast in a dress and heels?

"Run, Buck, run," Dewey called after him.

Thank God, she'd parked all the way in the back of the lot. Buck slammed against the side of Kermit just as Sunny reached the driver's side door. "Please," he said between huffs. "Wait—thank you."

Sunny stood stiffly with her back to him. "You're welcome. Is that all?"

"No!" He cleared his throat and lowered his voice, his breaths jagged. "I mean, could you wait a minute? I have some things to say."

She reached for the door handle. "Text me. I'm using my phone again."

Her cool tone brought his pulse down a notch. How could he explain the emotional rollercoaster ride he'd just taken? He took a deep breath. "Things okay with you and your mom?"

She finally looked at him. There were circles under her beautiful gold-flecked eyes. "Yes."

He sagged against the car, relieved. "Vince

said you two had worked it out. I was worried you might be putting on a show because of his heart condition."

Sunny shook her head. "It was hard. My mom and I finally talked through everything. I work here now, not at the shop."

"You okay with that?" he asked.

She nodded.

"Thank you for rescuing Gina," he said softly. He watched her pink lips round in surprise.

"Don't thank me," she said finally. "That was Tanya's idea. I just went along for the ride."

Buck was sure Sunny had done more than just gone along for the ride. "Dewey and I went looking for Gina. We found Carly Day instead." He shook his head, still stunned by what his mother had admitted. "She made sure Gina saw the unglamorous side of casino life. She asked a friend to assign Gina to work the kitchen night shift."

"Oh, my God," Sunny said, her voice barely audible.

"Tell me about it." His mother had destroyed all his previous assumptions about her selfishness with one selfless act. "I don't know how to reconcile the woman my mother has become with the woman she's been."

"Maybe that's not up to you," she said with a gentle smile. "Maybe that's better left in God's hands."

Buck gulped. "Is that what you've done with

me?" he asked, suddenly afraid of the answer. "Put me in God's hands?"

Sunny's chin quivered. "That's where we all are," she whispered.

The immensity of her simple words tore down the last bit of wall around his heart. It was true. The love of so many people, people he'd often run away from, had gotten him to this point. From the moment his grandmother had baptized him in a rusted-out trailer, his life, everything he'd done, had resulted from the kindness of others. How else could he explain rising above adversity, surviving abandonment, and building his own business? Lord knows, he didn't do anything to deserve it. He dropped to his knees in the grass.

Sunny knelt beside him. "What's wrong?" She clutched his arm, her worried gaze searching his face. "Are you sick?"

He shook his head. He wanted to laugh and shout with joy. Everything seemed so clear. So simple.

He gripped Sunny's hands. "I'm selling part of the business to Remy and moving back to Lilac. Norbert can live with me if he wants."

Sunny's smile beamed through the tears streaming down her cheeks.

"Please tell me I haven't blown it." He searched her face. "Can you forgive me for walking out like I did?"

She pressed his hand to her cheek and nodded.

Epilogue

Buck raked up the last stray leaves and stuffed them into the leaf bag. He inhaled the crisp October air, smiling as he tied the bag shut. Hefting the last load of leaves into his arms, he crossed the cleared labyrinth with a few quick steps and tossed it into the back of his Jeep. He stowed the rake and returned to the garden. He nodded as he surveyed the purple and yellow mums Father Dominic had planted.

The autumn winds had shaken the last of the leaves from the trees. Through the gaps in the branches, he could just make out Main Street and the front of the consignment shop his sister Gina now managed. There was still enough light in the sky to see the brightly colored clothes in the window. He'd been more than a little worried Gina might return to New Orleans after he'd announced he'd decided to make Remy and his brother his business partners by selling them forty percent of the eco-tour business. But she had surprised him and shown little interest in the news. She seemed to be happy now, fulfilled by the work she was doing and thinking of Lilac as home.

He thought of it as home now, too. Funny how that had happened. The house at the apple orchard still needed a lot of work, but it was livable. Comfortable enough for Norbert to spend the days with him and return to Mountain Mist in the evenings. It wouldn't be long before the place was all fixed up. He'd repaired those rickety front porch steps first thing, added a ramp to accommodate Norbert's walker, and extended the paved drive all the way up to the front porch. It tickled him to watch Norbert sitting in a lawn chair in the shade of a tree, inhaling the scent of apples that insisted on bursting to life on the twisted branches. This year the house, next year the orchard, he'd assured Norbert. He'd ordered every book he could find on raising apples and even spent time talking with farmers at the local co-op.

From boat captain to farmer. Talk about turning onto a different path.

The sun settled on top of the distant mountain ridge. He slipped his phone out of his shirt pocket to check the time. Maybe he should've asked Sunny to meet him earlier.

Sunny. She'd certainly stepped onto a different path. And talk about courage. She'd taken charge of her life and was moving in a whole new direction. She'd thrown herself into her coursework. Everyone loved her at Mountain Mist.

At the sound of rustling leaves, he turned. Sunny hurried towards him, wearing a fluffy wool sweater that almost reached the knees of her jeans, her dark hair swirling about her shoulders. He smiled at the sight of her beaten-up hiking boots, so different from the stylish shoes she typically wore. She'd come prepared to work.

"Sorry I'm late," she exclaimed before pressing a swift kiss to his lips. "Minor emergency. Mr. Zignetti's keyring got caught in Mrs. Skokel's wheelchair wheels. Don't ask."

Her cheeks were flushed from the cold, her eyes bright. She glanced around. "What happened to the leaves?"

"Already raked them up," he said as he took her hand and led her to a bench. "Thought maybe we could walk the labyrinth at sunset."

Sunny's brow furrowed as they sat. "Together? That's different."

"We can start a new trend." He pulled the small velvet box from his pocket and opened it. Sapphires and diamonds flashed in the late afternoon sun.

Sunny's hand flew to her cheek.

He got down on one knee. "It was my grandmother's," he said. "Norbert's been keeping it all these years."

He watched the play of emotions as her expression changed from surprise to outright shock. He gulped. Had he misread her feelings these past months?

"It's old-fashioned," he said quickly. "I know you're not crazy about antiques." His voice trailed off. How could he have forgotten what she'd said about the clutter in her parents' basement?

"Your grandmother wore this ring," she said, her voice soft.

He nodded.

"I love it," she said quietly, her gaze raising to his. "And I love you."

He exhaled the breath he'd been holding. "You'll marry me?"

"I'll marry you." She leaned forward and kissed him.

He could feel her smile against his lips.

"You do realize you'll be getting in-laws with this arrangement," she said, eyes flashing mischievously.

"Already spoke with them. We have their blessing." He stood and extended his hand. "I know big weddings take a lot of time to plan. I was thinking—"

Sunny shook her head and wrapped her arms around his waist. "No big wedding. I don't want to wait."

He tucked a lock of hair behind her ear. "What if I do?"

"What?" Her gaze shot to his face.

Confession time. "I've been meeting with Father Dominic. I'm becoming a Catholic in the spring."

Her jaw dropped. "You've been coming to church with me every Sunday. Why didn't you say something?" She looked at the ground and then back up at his face, her brows furrowed. "You're not doing this just for me, are you?"

"That's why I didn't tell you. I wanted to be

sure." He faced her. "I'd be lying if I said you weren't a part of my decision. But, no, I'm not doing this for you. I'm doing it for me."

Her lips relaxed into a smile. "I must say, the Lilac gossip mill is falling down on the job. Hard to believe no one told me." Her expression softened. "I still want a small wedding. You're a very private person."

He shook his head, loving her even more for being willing to have a small ceremony. "This is the first wedding I've ever looked forward to. I don't care if the whole world comes, as long as you're there." He wrapped his hand around hers. "Ready?"

Sunny laughed and rested her cheek on his shoulder as they entered the labyrinth together.

THE END

If you enjoyed True Hearts, you may enjoy Wings of Love. Read the first chapter here.

Chapter One

Too late to turn back now.

Sweat streamed down Jack's face as he jogged past dilapidated vehicles and boarded-up storefronts. The early May sun, unseasonably hot, beat down on his shoulders, burning the back of his neck. If it weren't for the gang-symbol graffiti and distant Washington, D.C. skyline, he could almost imagine himself back in a war zone.

Marco's men were posted along rooftops and slouching in doorways. Their hawk-like gazes had tracked him for three blocks, assessing the threat he posed. Maybe he should've brought another Peacetalker. But Marco's invitation had been explicit. Come alone.

He stopped in front of a ramshackle house and lifted the lower edge of his tee shirt to wipe the sweat from his face. See guys, no wire. No weapons.

"Come on," a male voice ordered from the dark interior.

He followed Marco's man through the dimly lit hall. The guy had missed his calling. With a build like that he could've easily been a professional linebacker. Or a Green Beret.

Thick curtains covered the windows. A group of young men sat crowded around a large flat screen television, engrossed in a first-person shooter game. Electronic explosions mingled with curses and verbal jibes as the players battled for dominance. Ash trays overflowed with cigarette butts. Empty pizza boxes and drink cans littered the floor. The scene wasn't all that different from a frat house.

Except these guys were criminals.

Marco sat in the corner, hunched over his laptop. The gang leader had the piercing eyes of a leopard, the quick movements of a feral cat who could dominate one second and disappear the next. A man like Marco never met anyone in the same place twice.

"Jackie, my man. Thank you for accepting my invitation. Sit down." The black-inked skulls and scrolls on Marco's tattoo-covered arms told the story of gang affiliations and repeat jail time. "Where you been keeping yourself?"

Jack straddled the chair, resting his forearms on the back. "Wherever Steve sends me."

"You need a new boss. I can always use a man who knows his way around an AK-47."

He'd told Marco about his past experience as an army negotiator the first time they'd been introduced. Building the fragile trust that existed between criminals and mediators meant sharing information. For Peacetalkers, there could be no hidden agenda, no personal stake in the outcome of any negotiation. The only goal was peace.

Marco leaned back and spread his arms. "So, who's making deliveries at the soup kitchen in my territory? Peacetalkers and I had a deal it was off limits."

Jack trained his gaze on Marco's face. If the gang leader lied, he'd see the evidence in his eyes. "I hear it's one of your men."

"No way. Anybody doing deals at Father Jim's?" Marco called to the young men seated around the TV.

At the sound of Marco's voice, gaming and shouting stopped. All heads whipped around. A dozen sets of eyes trained on their leader like a pack of hounds transfixed by the hunter's command. Each man shook his head in silent response.

Marco spread his hands. "See. Not my guys."

The men resumed playing.

"Diners are complaining," Jack continued, his tone intentionally flat. "The police wanted to post an officer during meal times but Father Jim refused. Won't even let them install a surveillance camera."

Marco smiled, flashing his gold grills. "Father Jim's got cred."

Jack nodded. The elderly priest insisted his soup kitchen served all God's children, not just the law-abiding ones. "Sounds like the Peacetalkers have more work to do."

"Then do it," Marco said, his tone dismissive as he looked down at his laptop.

Meeting adjourned. Not a head turned as Jack walked out.

Marco's bodyguard led Jack to the sidewalk. "Not everybody's here," the man muttered, his lips barely moving.

Jack stared into the distance, keeping his expression neutral. Message received.

"Later, man." He took off jogging, arriving twenty minutes later at the Metro parking garage where he'd left his pickup. His heart pounded as his truck crawled through city traffic. He'd clean up and head into the office. He needed to tell Steve the rumor they'd heard might be true. One of Marco's men could be selling drugs in the soup kitchen behind the gang leader's back.

Slipping into an empty parking slot, he raced into his apartment building and up the steps. Half way down the hallway he reached for his keys and froze. The hairs on the back of his neck stood up. He looked over his shoulder.

A young man dressed in black stepped out of the shadow. "You're looking for who's selling at the soup kitchen." The dim light revealed the sheen of sweat on his brow, the fire of anger in his dark eyes.

"Marco was already looking before he called me." Jack spoke in the steady monotone he'd been trained to use in tense situations. "Father Jim's is a drug-free zone. Everybody knows that."

Light flickered on the blade the young man held in his shaking hand. "Marco declared war on whoever's dealing there."

Jack wished suddenly for the gun he'd given up when he'd chosen to become a Peacetalker. "Let's go to the police together. You'll get a lighter sentence if—"

"You think Marco can't reach into jail and punish me?" the young man snapped. The knife flashed.

Jack leapt to the side. The men tumbled to the floor, kicking the walls as they struggled. He winced as the knife sliced through his shirt.

An apartment door opened and somebody yelled. His attacker jumped to his feet and ran. Head throbbing, Jack listened to a distant voice calling the police. He heard the sound of fluttering wings just before everything went black.

~

Reo Greene inhaled the fresh mountain breeze, the scent of lilacs tickling her nose. Main Street pulsed with the sound of pounding feet. She took a cup of water from the table in front of the library and offered it to a woman running past. "Great job! Way to go!"

She glanced down the street at the town hall clock. Not much longer and the race would be over. She took a deep breath and rolled her head from side to side, wincing at the tension in her neck. She'd put off her teaching methods research paper longer than she should have. But when she'd signed up to coordinate Lilac's first 5K race, she hadn't realized it was being held the weekend before final exams. Once she completed all the work for her online college classes, she could focus on practicing for her job interview. Everyone said she was a shoo-in for a teaching job at Lilac Mountain High School.

She looked around and smiled. She'd never seen Main Street so alive on a Saturday morning. The sleepy Virginia mountain town had been preparing for this day for months. Brick-front shop windows contained brightly colored displays. Spectators lined the sidewalks, cheering on friends and family members as they jogged past. She pulled out her phone and took some pictures for the town's social media page. She turned around to take a selfie with the finish line behind her.

Welcome Home, Jack Warfield!

The white welcome banner strung above Main Street billowed into her camera's view. She scowled. She'd heard Jack Warfield was coming back. Had won a medal and gotten out of the army.

With any luck, she wouldn't have to see him.

She lowered her phone and looked directly into the sympathetic gaze of Miss Emma, the town librarian.

The older woman stood at the next water table,

filling cups. "You're not worried about seeing Jack again, are you?"

My, oh my, Miss Emma didn't miss a trick. And she didn't think twice about saying exactly what was on her mind. Reo sniffed. "He should be worried about seeing me."

Miss Emma tilted her head. "Over five years have passed. Hope you two can let bygones be bygones."

Reo reached for an empty cup and filled it. "I won't start anything if he doesn't."

Miss Emma nodded her approval, then waved at a group of teenage runners. "Over four hundred participants. Can you believe it? Who said nobody would show up?"

Reo glanced around, studying the crowd. "It's hard to tell if there are more townies or more newcomers." Since the solar plant had opened a few years back, Lilac's modest population had almost doubled. Townies made a point of complaining about the crowds whenever they couldn't find a Main Street parking space or had to wait in line too long at Allen and Eva's Organic Produce.

Miss Emma continued to hand water to passing runners. "They're doing an activity together, that's the important thing. And the town has you to thank for coordinating it. That will look great on your resume." She nudged Reo's arm as Principal Owens and some of the high school teachers ran by and waved.

"I only organized it," Reo protested, waving back to her—fingers crossed—future boss and coworkers. "The race was your idea."

"You probably shouldn't say that too loudly." Miss Emma inclined her head towards Mayor Tom Burgin who stood at the finish line, high-fiving the runners. She frowned. "Bad enough the mayor pooh-poohed the race when I suggested it. Then he turned around and made it sound like his own idea at the next town council meeting. I tell you, my jaw hurt for a week from the tongue lashing I gave him." She patted Reo's hand. "But he made up for it by putting you in charge. The town can always trust you to do things right."

Reo bit her tongue. When she'd agreed to organize the race, she'd had no idea how much time it would take. With all the squabbling over how the event would impact Main Street businesses and other Saturday morning activities, you'd think she was coordinating an Olympic marathon. She picked up her clipboard and studied her checklist. She hadn't forgotten anything. If things continued to go smoothly, she'd be back working on her research paper before lunch.

Miss Emma's short silver curls bobbed in the breeze as she walked over to Reo's table. "Even before I told off Mayor Burgin at the town council meeting, he wasn't talking to me. We haven't had a pleasant conversation in years."

"How come?"

Miss Emma leaned against Reo's shoulder. "Honey, I'd tell you if I could remember." She burst out laughing.

"You ladies gonna let me in on the joke?" Lavinia Burgin tottered towards their table, diamond pendant glistening at the neckline of her bright pink jogging outfit. Wearing a matching diamond tennis bracelet and two massive diamond stud earrings, the mayor's wife was a walking advertisement for her jewelry shop, Sparkles Galore.

Miss Emma cleared her throat. "That sun is fierce. The mayor must be feeling hotter than a sun-scorched gecko. Think he might like a drink?"

Lavinia whirled around. "Oh, my goodness, his face is beet red. I told him to wear a hat!" She glanced at the steady stream of runners then down at her platform sandals. "Reo, honey, you're wearing sensible shoes. Be a darling and run a drink out to him."

Miss Emma extended a cup to Lavinia, eyebrows lifted. "Don't you think the mayor would prefer receiving a drink from his wife? Reo is not your gofer."

Lavinia scowled. "Honestly, Emma, I'm wearing four-inch heels. I'm just asking Reo to do me a favor."

Miss Emma held the cup steady. Lavinia refused to take it.

Reo pushed a stray lock out of her eyes and tucked it into her pony tail. Really? Miss Emma and Lavinia were going to start something now? It had been awkward enough growing up in a town where every adult female behaved as if she had a say in how Reo should be raised. She shot Miss Emma a please-don't-do-this look, took the cup, and smiled at Lavinia. "No problem. I'll take it to him."

She waited at the curb near the finish line, looking for a break in the runners. After a cluster of teenagers passed, she stepped into the street. "Here you go, Mayor—Oomph!"

The cup sailed out of her hand, splashing water into her eyes. Legs tangled with hers as her elbow connected with something hard. She heard a grunt as a pair of strong hands wrapped around her waist, steadying her while runners hurried past. The scent of orange juice and spicy, masculine soap washed over her. She blinked hard to clear her vision.

"You okay?" a male voice asked.

Jack Warfield's chiseled face hovered inches above hers. His dark-eyed gaze studied her, surprised. Hints of the rebel who'd left five years ago lingered at the edges of his wary expression. Muscled arms held her close like they had only one time before.

She gulped, her face warm, and squirmed out of his grasp. "I'm fine."

Sunlight glinted off the chestnut hair tumbling over his forehead. The corner of his mouth curled. "Wish I could say the same for the mayor."

She whirled around. Mayor Burgin had moved to the sidewalk. Lavinia stood beside him, pressing a paper towel to his cheek. The front of his red polo shirt was splattered with water.

"Oh, no." Reo wiped water from her cheeks as she dodged runners. "Mayor Burgin, I'm so sorry."

"It was my fault, sir." Jack joined them and extended his hand.

Her jaw dropped. Jack accepting the blame for something? That was new.

Mayor Burgin waved away the paper towel. "It'll dry, Lavinia. A little water never hurt anybody. You two okay?"

She'd just collided with the one guy who hated her guts so, no, not really. She nodded, silently commanding her heart to stop pounding.

Mayor Burgin gave Jack an appraising look then clasped his hand. "Welcome home, son. Couldn't believe my ears when your uncle Pete said you were coming back for a visit." He turned to Reo. "Where are we on the schedule?"

She whirled around in a sudden panic. "Where's my clipboard?"

Jack extended his hand. "You dropped this."

Fighting the urge to grab it from him, she accepted it with a tight smile. "Thank you." She flipped through the pages while her heart galloped. Everything had been going so smoothly before Jack showed up.

She cleared her throat. "So far, so good. Filmore Hardware wants the sidewalk cleared by nine-thirty so they can put out their mowers and wheelbarrows. The flower shop can't display all their carts until we break down the stage. St. Andrew's has a wedding at eleven and needs parking space for the limo. As long as the runners finish by nine-fifteen, we should be fine."

Mayor Burgin glanced at the race clock. "Perfect. Jack, when I go on stage to announce the winners, I'd like to introduce you to the crowd, officially welcome you back, and tell the story of how you got your medal. How does that sound?"

"Thanks for the offer," Jack replied, his expression polite, "but I'd rather not."

"What?" Lavinia squawked, dropping the roll of paper towels.

Reo choked back a startled laugh. Jack shot her a sideways glance before retrieving the paper towel roll from the sidewalk and offering it to the mayor's wife. Lavinia snatched it from his grasp with a huff.

The mayor nodded, his expression serious. "Understood. Served two tours overseas myself." He waved a thumb at the welcome home banner. "How about that thing?"

Reo waited as Jack studied the banner, his

expression unreadable.

"The banner was a real surprise," he said finally.

Lavinia squeezed the mayor's arm and squealed, "See, I told you he'd like it."

Mayor Burgin patted his wife's hand. His thoughtful gaze moved to Reo's face then back to Jack's. "I have a project I'd like to discuss with you two. Come by my office on Monday. Say around eleven?"

A project? She'd just finished organizing a 5K race. Reo pulled out her phone and checked her calendar. Her research paper was due by nine Monday morning. She didn't have to be at her part-time job at the DMV until after lunch. "Works for me."

Jack cleared his throat. "If you don't mind my asking, sir, what's this about?"

"Rather not discuss it here. We'll chat Monday." Mayor Burgin winked. "Almost time to announce the winners. Reo, please meet Lavinia and me at the stage area with the results."

"Okay." She waited until they left and turned to Jack. "Still stirring up trouble, I see."

"What? Saying no to the mayor or running into you?" He lifted the edge of his tee shirt to wipe the perspiration from his face.

"Did you run into me on purpose?" she challenged, refusing to let his muscled abs distract her.

He lowered his shirt and cocked his head. "You think I ran into you on purpose?"

She raised her chin. She'd be darned if he would push her around this time. "Did you?"

"Jack!" Miss Emma waved from her spot behind the water table. "Come over here so I can get a good look at you."

Reo crossed her arms, waiting.

His gaze moved from the top of her head to the toes of her running shoes and back up. "I did not run into you on purpose," he said finally. "But keep up the attitude and you'll make me wish I had." He strode across the sidewalk and engulfed the librarian's tiny frame in a tender hug.

Reo's heart pounded as she watched a small crowd form around him. Townies who remembered Jack from his high school football days slapped him on the back and shook his hand. Women fluttered around him like hummingbirds, drinking in his all-American good looks. The breath eased out of her lungs. Jack did not intimidate her any more. She didn't care what he thought about her. She'd been in the right at that party. He was the one who'd been out of line.

The town hall clock struck nine. Pushing thoughts of Jack out of her mind, she trotted over to the timekeeper's table, snatched up the results, and hurried to the stage where Mayor Burgin waited. "Here you go!"

The mayor took the results and walked to the podium. Lavinia stood beaming at his side as he began his remarks. The crowd gathered around the stage, faces bright and attentive.

Reo felt a tug on her sleeve. She turned around to see the stooped back of Mrs. Newmacher, motioning for her to follow.

"Would you help me?" Mrs. Newmacher asked over her shoulder as she shuffled towards Sweet Blossoms, her florist shop. Her wrinkled hand brushed the gray bangs out of her eyes. "I want to put out some flower baskets while folks are still milling around. Potential sales, you know."

Reo shot a look at the stage where the mayor was speaking. She wanted to hear him announce the winners, but how could she say no to Mrs. Newmacher? "Sure." She followed the florist into the shop, lifted two of the hanging baskets, and carried them to the sidewalk. Mrs. Newmacher pointed to the hooks where she wanted Reo to hang the pink and white petunias.

"I'll roll out the flower carts after they take down the stage, just like we agreed," Mrs. Newmacher said when they finished hanging half a dozen baskets. She stood back and admired the display. "I don't know why anyone would decorate with balloons or plastic streamers when they could use vibrant, natural blossoms."

Reo glanced at the red, white, and blue balloon arch covering the finish line and frowned. Was Mrs. Newmacher talking about the race decorations? Who ever heard of hanging flowers over a finish line?

The florist turned an admiring eye to her shop window where lush lilac blossoms cascaded from a wicker basket. A heart-shaped lavender sign reminded customers to purchase flowers for Mother's Day. Only one day left.

Reo looked away.

"Flowers make the best decorations, don't you agree?" Mrs. Newmacher asked.

Reo flipped through the papers on her clipboard. "They certainly are pretty."

"Let's have a round of applause for all the volunteers who made this day possible," the mayor said over the loudspeaker. "Special thanks to Reo Greene for taking the lead and making everything run smoothly."

Her cheeks warmed as the folks around her smiled and clapped.

Mrs. Newmacher rested her wrinkled hand on Reo's shoulder. "Thank you for your help, dear." She shuffled back into her shop.

Country music played over the loudspeakers as the mayor left the podium. The high school coaches got to work disassembling the stage and loading the parts into pickup trucks. Reo texted herself a reminder to send thank you notes to the high school band instructor for lending the portable stage and to all the coaches for setting it up and tearing it down. Between finishing her paper, completing her final exams, and preparing for her job interview, her schedule was going to be crazy this week. She'd feel so much better once she got the call from Lilac Mountain High School with her interview time.

"Rhiannon Greene," a female voice boomed over the music. "Drop the clipboard and put your hands up."

Reo whirled around.

Her best friend Sunny DeStefano stood in the middle of Main Street, directing traffic with a megaphone and pointing at her. Wearing an orange construction vest over her swirly pink sun dress, Sunny held up a manicured hand to stop pedestrians as a row of pickup trucks backed into the lane. Once all the trucks pulled away, she waved the pedestrians across the street and scurried to the sidewalk. "Let the traffic begin!" she called through the megaphone, motioning for the waiting cars to move.

"Look at that. Plenty of time before the limo arrives." Sunny fluffed her long dark hair off her shoulders. A single neon-pink-dyed curl curved around her right cheek. "My mom just texted me. She's doing hair at the bride's house. The family's going nuts, worrying the race won't be over in time for the limo to park in front of St. Andrew's."

Reo sank onto a wrought iron bench, overcome with relief as the crowd mingled around them. The race was over. She'd done it. "Thanks for taking charge of clean-up."

"Because I'm so good at ordering people around? One of the secret powers I inherited from my mother." Sunny spread the hem of her skirt and did a mini curtsy before dropping onto the bench. "You had the harder job. Convincing all these Main Street business owners to even have a race. I'd have no patience for that."

"If anyone says another word about blocking ATM access or interfering with yoga studio ambiance, shoot me." Reo fought the wave of exhaustion that washed over her, stifling a yawn. "I barely slept last night, worrying something would go wrong."

"You worry too much." Sunny pulled off the orange construction vest and folded it. "Although my mom did want to call you at five a.m. this morning. She was mad about the race clock being set up in front of the salon. I had to wrestle the phone out of her hand and hide it."

Reo glanced over at the Up Do salon where volunteers were taking down the clock. "Do you think I did okay?"

"Aside from not wearing that cute white denim skirt you bought last week for the race?"

Reo's hand flew to her cheek. "I completely forgot." She glanced down at her oversized Ridgeland College tee shirt, bike shorts, and running shoes. "I got up so early, I pulled on the first thing I saw."

Sunny shrugged. "Considering you spilled water all over the mayor, it's probably good you didn't wear the new skirt."

Reo cringed. "You saw that."

"Couldn't miss it." Sunny's gaze narrowed. "I also saw Jack Warfield bump into you."

Reo crossed her arms, remembering his crack about her attitude. "He's still mad at me."

Sunny snorted. "You'd think he'd be over it by now."

"You'd think." Reo rolled her eyes. "Any idea why the mayor wants to meet with Jack and me Monday morning?"

"Together?" Sunny scrunched up her face then snapped her fingers. "Maybe he wants you two to end your feud."

Reo looked towards the library where a crowd of folks still stood talking with Jack. "There's no feud. He just blames me for destroying his chance to go to college."

"Like he needed help with that." Sunny's phone dinged. She shoved the megaphone into Reo's hands and jumped to her feet. "Mom ran out of hair spray. Are we done?"

Reo glanced around. Runners and spectators mingled around the storefronts, munching on the after-race snacks set out by each shop. The stage was gone. The water tables had been cleared and put away. Traffic was flowing again which meant she could go home and get to work on her paper. She nodded. "The firemen will take down the balloon arch later this evening. Thanks again for helping." She waved to Sunny, then stretched out her legs and yawned. Her first moment of peace since before dawn. The breeze felt so nice. She'd enjoy it for a few minutes and then—

"Reo!" a male voice barked. "What is this mess?"

She jerked up straight and looked around.

Allen Owens of Allen and Eva's Organic Produce stood outside the entrance of his store, his arm extended in a rigid line. Dressed in denim overalls and a plaid shirt, he pointed his index finger at a group of metal folding chairs stacked in front of his strawberry stand. "We talked about this. Our customers must have easy access to the produce at all times."

"The pickup trucks will be back in just a few minutes."

Allen raised his eyebrows and shook his head. "I need these chairs moved now."

"All right." She rose to her feet. So much for relaxing.

~

Jack frowned at the welcome banner. The simple flyer he'd spotted outside the convenience store last night had made the race sound like a community fun run. Just the thing to blow off steam after the week he'd had. No wonder the folks at the registration table had been so friendly when he'd signed in. He'd stumbled when he noticed his name hanging above the finish line, his misstep propelling him straight into Reo Greene.

Now, as a result of that banner announcing his return, a group of residents crowded around him.

"When'd you arrive in town?" a woman standing beside him asked.

He smiled politely. "Last night."

"See any action?" an older gentleman chimed in.

"In Lilac?" Jack deadpanned. "No, sir."

After the laughter died down, another man asked, "Where were you stationed?"

Reminded him of somebody, but darn if he could remember who. "Split my time between the Middle East and Texas."

"Your Texas unit earned the medal for the hostage rescue, right?"

"Yes, sir." Jack nodded.

The man patted him on the back. "Two heroes in one family. Always knew you'd follow in your father's footsteps."

Had the sun on his face gotten hotter? "Just doing my duty." Jack's gaze strayed over the crowd, honed in on Reo, her blond ponytail swaying as she talked on her cell phone. Of all the people he could have collided with, why did it have to be her? Annoyance shot through him as memories of senior year came rushing back. He'd hated her for what she'd done the night of that party. And it was clear from the way she'd pushed out of his arms this morning that she was still angry at him, too.

"When did you get out of the army?" a woman who reminded him of somebody from his mother's former garden club asked.

"Six months ago."

"What're you doing now?" she asked.

"Working in Washington as a conflict mediator." And he'd be doing it right now if he weren't on a leave of absence. Another thing he hadn't seen coming.

"How's your momma doing?" a man asked.

"Very well, sir. She lives with her sister in Tampa. They own a yarn shop."

"What are your plans, son?"

"Right now?" Jack asked. "Get used to being back in Lilac."

"That should take all of ten minutes. Then what?"

"Put my mother's rental property on the market. The tenants moved out and Mom's decided to sell."

"Sell? You're not gonna move in?"

Something pointed poked his palm. A brunette wearing a sleek green dress folded his fingers over a business card. "If you need a real estate agent, you know who to call." She flashed a bright smile at him.

"Yes, ma'am." He'd definitely seen her face before. Wasn't she the mother of one of his high school buddies?

"Been looking for you! There's a '69 Mustang in the shop you've got to see." Pete Warfield sidled into the group and slapped Jack on the back.

Pain shot through his shoulder. Direct hit on the stitches. He flinched as Pete pulled him into a bear hug, exhaling slowly when his uncle released him. Good ol' Pete. His thinning hair seemed grayer, but a good-natured smile still lit up his weathered features. They said their good-byes to the group and headed down the sidewalk.

Pete hitched up his jeans and turned to his nephew as soon as they were out of ear shot. "Aren't you gonna thank me for rescuing you?"

"Sure. Right after I thank you for telling everyone I was coming back. Not."

"I may have mentioned to Tom Burgin you were coming back. But don't blame me for that banner. That was Lavinia's idea. Tom would have an easier time stopping a speeding locomotive than saying no to Lavinia." Pete shook his head. "The woman would tie bows on every door knob if the town council would let her get away with it."

"So much for slipping quietly into town."

"You think that was even an option? Lavinia wanted to give you a parade." Pete chuckled. "Best to get the welcome home stuff over with as quickly as possible. Like ripping off a bandage."

The men walked out of the bright sun into the cool interior of Warfield's Garage. Jack inhaled the familiar scent of car polish and engine oil. He'd spent countless hours hanging out here as a kid, shooting the breeze with the uncle who'd taught him how to fix a flat and jump-start a battery. He whistled at the sight of the cherry-red convertible. "Sweet."

Pete nodded. "Belongs to one of the managers at the solar plant. Brings it here for tune-ups."

Jack circled the car, drinking in the details. A rich man's toy. "Good choice, since you're old enough to remember when the original model came out," he said with a grin.

Pete rested his hand on the hood. "They don't make 'em like they used to. Cars or men."

What did that mean? "Business must be good at the plant," Jack continued. "None of the guys I grew up with could afford a vehicle like this."

"No kidding."

"Any idea why Mayor Burgin wants to see me and Reo Greene in his office Monday morning?"

"You *and* Reo?" Pete's brows shot up. He rubbed the back of his neck. "The mayor might've said something about an opening on the town council."

Jack snorted. "Nice try. Told you. I'm not moving back to Lilac."

Pete fixed him with a serious look. "Your mother thinks you're risking your life for people who don't even want your help."

Jack stared at the grease-stained concrete floor and counted to ten. His mother had made it perfectly clear she thought he was wasting his talents working as a Peacetalkers' mediator. "If everyone believed that, all the violence in the world would never stop. You agree with her?"

"Don't know much about big city gangs," Pete said. "Just think it would be nice for you to come home. Take over the garage so it stays in the family."

Jack leaned a hip against the worktable. "Should've thought about that before you became a confirmed bachelor."

Pete's eyes flashed. He pointed at the sepia-toned photograph on the wall. "Your Great-Grandpa Warfield built this garage almost a century ago. Doesn't that mean anything to you?" He shook his head, his expression disappointed. "Had the same conversation with your father."

And if he'd listened, he might still be alive. His father had wanted nothing to do with the family business. He'd joined the army, chased adventure, and died a hero. "I gotta go. Get out of these sweaty clothes."

Pete turned away, busied himself rearranging the tools on his worktable. The whir of the overhead fan filled the awkward silence.

Jack blew out a breath. "How about breakfast tomorrow?"

"Yeah, sure." Pete didn't look up.

Jack pushed his hair out of his eyes. He'd pissed off

his uncle, been lassoed by the mayor for some mysterious project, and collided with the one girl who despised him. Maybe hunkering down in Lilac until this leave of absence business blew over wasn't the best plan of action after all.

Pamela Ferguson is the author of sweet romances set in small towns. Specializing in gossips, meddlers, matchmakers and happily-ever-afters, Pam loves dreaming up complications that wreak havoc in the lives of her characters. Her determined heroes and resourceful heroines are forever doing battle with narrow-minded mischief makers. Who knew there were so many bumps on the road to love?

When she isn't writing, Pamela can be found teaching English, reading, and travelling. She and her husband of thirty-four years are empty nesters, which means they have a lot of time to devote to their high-energy German shepherd puppy and mischievous orange tabby. She loves to hear from readers. Drop her a line at pam@pamelaferguson.com.

Social Media:
Facebook:
https://www.facebook.com/PamelaFergusonAuthor/
Twitter: @pfwrites
Website: pamelaferguson.com
Pinterest:www.pinterest.com/pfwrites
Goodreads: pamelaferguson@outlook.com
Instagram: @pfwrites

www.ingramcontent.com/pod-product-compliance
Lightning Source LLC
Chambersburg PA
CBHW072258130726
47910CB00012B/2126